THE
PERFECT
LIAR

THE
PERFECT
LIAR

Thomas Christopher Greene

ST. MARTIN'S PRESS NEW YORK

This is a work of fiction. All of the characters, organizations, and events portrayed in this novel are either products of the author's imagination or are used fictitiously.

www.stmartins.com

Designed by Steven Seighman

Library of Congress Cataloging-in-Publication Data

Names: Greene, Thomas Christopher, 1968– author.
Title: The perfect liar : a novel / Thomas Christopher Greene.
Description: First edition. | New York : St. Martin's Press, 2019.
Identifiers: LCCN 2018029125| ISBN 9781250128218 (hardcover) |
ISBN 9781250128041 (ebook)
Subjects: | GSAFD: Suspense fiction.
Classification: LCC PS3607.R453 P47 2019 | DDC 813/.6—dc23
LC record available at https://lccn.loc.gov/2018029125

Our books may be purchased in bulk for promotional, educational, or business use. Please contact your local bookseller or the Macmillan Corporate and Premium Sales Department at 1-800-221-7945, extension 5442, or by email at MacmillanSpecialMarkets@macmillan.com.

First Edition: January 2019

10 9 8 7 6 5 4 3 2 1

For Sarah, the reason I do everything

THE
FIRST
NOTE

MUCH LATER WHAT SUSANNAH WILL remember about that morning is the rain, that warm May rain, how it felt on her bare arms when she ran, how it matted her long ginger hair to her head, how it smelled like freshly cut grass, how it sounded falling in sheets off the roof of the empty house.

Outside of the rain, the morning was quite ordinary. A Tuesday, the spring of 2014. Her husband, Max, was in Chicago giving a talk at the Art Institute. Freddy, her son, overslept slightly and then scarfed down three bowls of cereal before running out the door with his backpack on and his skateboard under his arm, barely stopping to say goodbye before stepping out into the rain. Susannah was left with the whole day as big and as empty as a lake in front of her.

She made herself a cappuccino with the Nespresso machine that she and Max had recently bought and that they were in love with. They wondered how they had lived without it. It was like being a barista without any of the fuss or the mess. After, she sat on the screened-in back porch and sipped her coffee and watched the rain. The large green backyard was lined with peonies about to bloom, so beautiful, she thought, and Susannah looked at them and then back into the house, to the wide rooms with the polished wood floors, and she sighed pleasantly, and not for the first time, as if remembering the whirlwind of good fortune that had led the three of them to this grand old house on a hill above Lake Champlain in Burlington, Vermont, nine months before.

Sometimes life changes in an instant, doesn't it? One minute she's a single mom, and then she meets an amazing man who literally rocks her world, and then his career, surprising both of them, takes off like a red-hot rocket. It felt like yesterday that she was introducing him to her boss at the gallery, and within months Max's handsome mug is on the cover of all the important art magazines. The challenge was that he didn't really make anything—the heart of his work was his ability to talk—so there was no obvious way to monetize it. The irony was that now you could become an art-world star and not sell paintings for millions of dollars. It was less about what you made than who you were.

Max gave a TED Talk that went viral. No one had ever talked about art this way before. He was in demand to give it everywhere. Shortly thereafter, a number of universities called with luxurious job offers. Vermont was the obvious choice. Kansas sounded dreadful (*Who wants to live in Kansas?* Max wondered) and so did the offer from the university in Atlanta, with all the imagined heat and the lack of seasons. But the clincher was when in the small galley kitchen in their apartment in the Village, Max said, "Here's the best part, Susannah, look at this."

He pulled out his phone and showed her the picture of this house. It was stunning, the kind of house she never imagined she would live in.

"They give us this house," he said.

"Give it to us?"

"Well, *give* is a strong word. But it's a three-year appointment and it's ours during that time."

Susannah shrieked, a real one, shrieked and hugged him hard, hugged him for his charm and talent, for how much people gravitated to him and wanted to see whatever he wanted to happen to happen, how he could will things into being, but she also hugged him because three years sounded beautifully long, long enough to get Freddy out of the city through high school. The thought of him no longer vanishing into Union Square Park with a skateboard and a hacky sack, and into the vast city where the lines between childhood and adulthood were often blurred, was almost enough to make Susannah giddy.

She stood and moved off the porch and into the wide-open living room and then into the kitchen, where she left her coffee mug in the sink next to the cereal bowl still full of milk that Freddy had deposited there hours ago.

It was time for her run. She always had this brief moment before she went when she had to will herself and imagine doing it, her legs churning as she propelled herself down the hill. Susannah didn't believe those who said they loved to run, though she believed it when they said that they loved how running made them feel after it was over.

As always, she had to remind herself that the run was not a choice for her. Years ago during an episode, a therapist had said, "I have lots of tricks to help you, Susannah, but nothing will help you as much as vigorous exercise. You need to do it every day."

Once outside, she loved the rain. She stood for a minute just looking at the quiet neighborhood, the neighborhood in repose, like a beautiful woman sleeping, everyone at work, rows and rows of stately Victorians on a flat stretch of hill, the lake blurry with mist below. She let the rain just fall on her, warm and soft, sweet-smelling rain, and when her hair was soaked and her bare arms were wet, she went.

In New York, Susannah would run along the crowded walkway

next to the Hudson, and she always kept her focus on the river, the rise of the chop and the tugboats and barges moving along it. This was her strategy for ignoring the eyes on her, the men who shamelessly stared at the rise and fall of her tits and the curve of her ass under her black tights.

She wore earphones so no one would try to speak to her. Even in Vermont she wore the earphones, phone hooked to her waist, but here they didn't stare so blatantly.

Her route took her out of the neighborhood and then down the main street to the lakefront, and along that great expanse of water, the row of bluish mountains on the other side.

Then back the way she came, the last leg the hardest, straight uphill, her muscles straining, and she could taste that cigarette she would reward herself with on her return. She only smoked a couple every day, but she looked forward to them with the reverence of a religious ritual. It was a small indulgence, Susannah liked to tell herself, and given the air up here, no different from being a nonsmoker in the city. Or so someone had once told her and she had latched on to it like gospel.

Coming back up her street, she slowed. She was breathing hard. Two houses before hers, as she always did, she started to walk, her hands on her hips, shaking her legs out in front of her.

The rain picked up even more and it felt great. Finally stopping in front of her house, Susannah lifted her face to it, letting the rain hit her forehead, her cheeks, her mouth, practically drinking all that rain.

In that moment she noticed the note. It was taped to the front door. At first Susannah didn't think that it was anything at all—this was a neighborhood where people left notes, so unlike New York. Usually someone announcing a yard sale or a block party, or just that everyone—meaning all the couples of the same age group who lived in the "hood," as they called it—was getting together on this or that porch for drinks after the kids fell asleep.

Susannah stretched. She reached above her head, then bent down and touched her toes, liking the feel of her hamstrings as they strained. Standing back erect, she moved to the house, up the porch, and, almost as an afterthought, grabbed the note off the door.

Inside the house, Susannah opened it, and there, written in blocky black letters on thick cardstock paper, she read:

I KNOW WHO YOU ARE

She stopped and read it again. Her heart, elevated already from the run, began to race. A feeling of dread swept over her, a feeling that she recognized from long ago. Suddenly she was afraid that her motor, as she called it, would start to run and the panic would rise faster than a tide within her, and this would be the time she wouldn't be able to beat it back.

Susannah looked back to the door, then to the windows on either side of it. She went to the door and locked it. Then she turned around and started to shout into her own house, like someone walking through the woods might do so as to not startle a bear.

"Hello," Susannah yelled. "The police are on their way."

But the house greeted her with silence. A silence she didn't trust.

Susannah ran around and locked all the doors—the door to the back porch, the sliding ones that lead out to the back patio, and even the latch to the basement. It was so different here from in New York. In Vermont, after the first week, they had stopped locking their doors, except at night and out of habit. Their small garden apartment in Manhattan had no less than six locks; it was like opening a vault. Metal grates were on the windows. Anyone off the street could try to break in, but good luck.

She raced through the house, running up the wide wooden staircase with its big landing before it curved right and up to the hallway and the bedrooms. She shouted as she went, having no idea what to expect but wanting to know the place was empty. For a minute, Susannah wanted to feel safe.

In the bedroom she shared with Max, she opened the closet, looked into the bathroom, nervously peeled away the shower curtain, half expecting someone to jump out at her while she movie-screamed in the person's face.

She went into Freddy's room, cluttered and full of graphic novels in stacks like magazines and the crazy disarray that said in bright orange neon that a fifteen-year-old lived here: his clothes and crap in piles everywhere. She peered into his closet, too.

Susannah accepted that she was alone. Downstairs in the kitchen, she found her pack of American Spirit cigarettes and the lighter in their hiding spot in the high cabinet above the fridge.

She looked outside to the blue rain falling steadily, and instead of going out under the eaves—her usual spot—she told herself, *Fuck it,* and turned the crank on the two windows above the sink to open them, and with her hands shaking, she lit a cigarette, hoping the smell would be gone by the time Freddy returned home.

Susannah smoked furtively, the way mental patients do. Pulling hard and fast with the cigarette between pursed lips. The smoke swirled up above her face in thin plumes and she waved at it, a futile attempt to brush it away, to make it disappear.

Inside, though, she was starting to roil, and she had to remind herself that the anxiety was what she thought of as a white bear, and it was okay to have white bears. It was okay to think of the white bear, even when you were not supposed to. The white bear can only bite if you try to ignore its existence. Men fear death, she told herself, while women fear something far worse: losing their minds.

And fear, when you got right down to it, was the most natural thing in the world.

THREE YEARS BEFORE SUSANNAH FOUND the first note on the door in Vermont, Max crashed the party. Max had gone there with a single purpose, explicitly to seduce her, though he didn't know who *her* was, or if there would be a her, and he certainly hadn't counted on falling in love with Susannah, for Max wasn't sure he was capable of that kind of love. Nothing in his life to that point suggested it was possible.

This happened in the winter, a few days before Valentine's Day. Seemingly every storefront in Manhattan was displaying giant red bows. It snowed. A fluffy white New York snow that looked pretty but, when it fell, made the sidewalks and the street corners a slushy mess.

That morning Max had been working, taking down a show at a gallery in Chelsea, when the owner, Robert Williams, a semifamous figure who, when he walked through, barely looked at Max as if Max were the janitor sweeping the floor, got into a conversation with Davis, the manager who had hired Max a few weeks before. They were only a few feet from Max and it was easy for him to eavesdrop.

Lydia Garabedian, the most famous art dealer in the world, was having a party that night at her Upper West Side apartment. Pretty much anyone who was anyone in the art world was expected to attend. Robert Williams, who was in his early seventies, had been invited, but Davis had not. Davis asked Williams if he was going.

"Past my bedtime, I'm afraid," Robert Williams said. Within a year he would be dead at the hand of his beloved cigarettes, and as he said this, he laughed his distinctive throaty laugh.

So that night Max dressed in his art-world finest, black jeans and black T-shirt, white sneakers, and over this he wore a peacoat and a black watch cap on his bald head. Looking in the mirror before heading out into the snow, though, he realized he looked like a stevedore in some old Brando movie, so he stopped and threw a red scarf around his neck for a bit of color. He then rode the subway to Seventy-second Street and walked east to Central Park West.

This part of New York, with its wide avenues and its stately pre-war buildings, the giant island of a park across the way, the trees that lined it painted white with new sticky snow, might as well have been a different country from Alphabet City, where Max lived. It felt big and rich and old as he walked north toward the San Remo, the iconic building where Lydia lived.

When he reached the front of it, Max stood for a moment and looked up at its great granite façade, the two towers that rose up near the top and loomed over the park. He had heard a story that in the 1960s Warren Beatty lived in one of the towers with whatever girlfriend he had at that time, and some famous actress lived in the other tower, and at night Mr. Beatty would move from tower to tower, from lover to lover. Max didn't know if that was true, but it was all he knew about the building before he walked into it that night. Other than that, he didn't belong there.

When Max approached the door, he pretended to be on his phone. The doorman looked at him slightly quizzically, and Max mouthed, "Lydia Garabedian," and the doorman opened the door and pointed him to a table in the lobby where two security guards sat behind a desk.

On his pretend phone call, Max was talking to a cab company, describing the fictional cab that had just dropped him off and in which he had left his wallet in the backseat. He said this all rather loudly and with much exasperation as he walked to the desk where the two men, both of them black and middle-aged and heavyset, sat staring at him blankly.

"Okay, okay," Max said to his fake phone call. "There is a reward for its safe return."

He hung up the fake call and looked at the two men. "Sorry about that, left my wallet in the cab. What a nightmare."

"Can we help you?" one of them said.

"I'm here for Lydia Garabedian."

"Name?"

"Robert Williams."

The one who hadn't spoken looked at a clipboard in front of him. He ran a pencil down a list of names and found that one. "We just need some photo ID."

"Well, that's the thing. I don't know if you heard me on the phone, but I left my wallet in the cab. Sorry. But if you want, Lydia is an old friend, I'm sure she would come down—"

They looked at each other. Max knew this was not a palatable choice. One of them handed him a small card and said, "This is for the elevator. Hold it up to the black mirror outside the elevators. Go through these two rooms behind me and the elevator is there."

Max nodded and took the card and walked past them and into an ornate ballroom, dimly lit and entirely empty, with a ceiling that rose up in ribbons like being underneath a tent, and painted a deep red, like something you might see in a Turkish palace. The floors were marble and his sneakers squeaked as he walked across them and into the other room, virtually identical, though smaller, and what had been red was now the pale blue of a robin's egg.

Max was thinking how oddly empty the whole place seemed when a couple moved toward him from the room where the elevator must be, and as they passed, a pretty blonde and an older man, Max recognized the man as Alec Baldwin, the actor, looking harried as if he was late for a plane, and Max thought, *Indeed, you are in a different New York*.

The elevator room was long and narrow and high ceilinged. A bank of elevators stood all in a row, no buttons, but there, in the middle of them, was a black mirror, and he took the card he had been given and held it up to it, and just like that the elevator to his right shot open. He stepped in, and inside, the back wall was mirrored and the rest of it was fine dark wood, and again there were no buttons. The elevator door closed and the elevator began to rise smoothly and quickly up.

He had no way of knowing what floor it took him to. But when the door opened, to his surprise it opened directly into Lydia's living room. He wasn't fully prepared for this, having imagined gathering his thoughts in the hallway before knocking on a door. He had wanted a chance to collect himself, smile widely, since he was about to pull off a piece of performance art.

Instead, Max was thrust into it. People were everywhere, lounging on couches, standing in small packs, in a line at the bar. Long windows looked out to the snowy park, and straight ahead he got a sense of vertigo as he saw the street far below.

Max stepped forward, and a small Asian man confronted him, motioning for his coat and his hat and his scarf, all of which Max took off and handed to him.

Max eyed the bar, against the far wall, and his plan was to get over there, grab a drink, and then blend in. But suddenly in front of him was a woman, petite and curvy in a bright, fitted red dress, red hair expertly cut to her shoulders, a Roman nose and slightly olive skin, looking up at him with big butterscotch eyes.

"Hello." She held out her hand. "I'm Susannah."

"Max." He took her hand in both of his, a newly practiced gesture, looking her in the eye.

"Max?"

"Max W."

"Just *W*? Is that short for something?"

"It used to be."

"Well, you are mysterious, Max W. Can I get you a drink?" In her voice now Max heard the trace of an accent, European, Spanish maybe, and the way she said his name, the focused enunciation on her tongue, felt vaguely sexual.

"Do you work here?"

"I work for Lydia. Come, the bar is this way."

The room contained a particular class of New York intelligentsia, some of whom he recognized. All the novelists from Brooklyn named Jonathan were here, with their blocky glasses, and that ancient *New Yorker* art critic held court in one corner. And there was Lydia herself, instantly recognizable, seated on a white couch near the large window overlooking the park with her latest protégé, a young black graffiti artist who went by the moniker G Spot, sitting handsomely next to her.

Lydia, according to one of the art rags, had discovered him tagging in a subway and started him working on canvas. He was the latest It boy and was for the obvious reasons being pitched by her as the next Basquiat.

"Let me buy you a drink," Max said to Susannah as they reached the bar.

"They are free."

"I know that."

The bartender, who looked like a male model, with brushed-back black hair and the perfect five o'clock shadow, a white dress shirt with the sleeves rolled halfway up his impressive biceps—*Curls for girls*, Max thought—handed them each a glass of champagne.

As they stepped away from the bar, Max held his glass to hers. "Cheers."

They moved toward the far wall, less crowded, where a painting caught Max's eye. From one of the books that he had studied for moments exactly like this, he recognized it, an early de Kooning, a famous painting of a woman, slightly cubist in its inspiration, and as they moved close to it, Max saw that even though it was sixty or more years old, the paint still looked wet, as if the artist himself, long dead, had made those oil brushstrokes hours ago.

"Are you an artist?" Susannah asked him.

"Yes."

"Ah, I took you for a filmmaker."

"How come?"

"The all-black," she said with a sweep of her hand, taking in his body.

He laughed. "No. But can you imagine having this in your house?"

Now it was her turn to laugh. "You haven't seen the half of it."

"I imagine not."

"How do you know Lydia?"

"Well, I shouldn't tell you this. But I don't."

"But you got invited."

He leaned in close to her, though he didn't have to, the room was full of voices and noise, the low undercurrent of piped-in jazz that he had not heard until now. "Can you keep a secret?"

"That depends."

"Don't call security, but I am crashing."

It was a gambit, this honesty, but if she took it, which he hoped she would, it was the kind of thing that could bring them together. Max looked her right in the eyes and they were astonishing, her eyes, such a deep golden brown and big. She did not look away but instead leaned up toward him with her soft, accented voice and said, "Why are you doing that?"

"I wanted to meet Lydia."

"Well, you are about to do that, it appears."

And there was Lydia Garabedian, sliding up silently next to the two of them, her signature gray hair cut into a bob, her small dark eyes, her clothes, also a signature, white and flowing and loose.

"Susannah, who is this?"

Before Susannah could answer, Max pivoted so that he faced Lydia, and he looked down at this tiny woman who ruled the art world, who gave Jeff Koons, they said, the idea for the balloon sculptures, and who once told Damien Hirst that he should think about something primitive, a shark perhaps. For two decades she had been the great arbiter of taste for an entire universe of opinion.

"Max W."

She tilted her head slightly as if taking this in. "I think I've heard of you." Max did his best not to smile at this, since it was impossible. "Though I can't remember where. What is it you make?"

"I used to be a painter. Now I play with words and people."

"So you're a writer?"

"No, I am an artist. It is complicated. When the time is right, I would like to show you more. But I have to ask you, since you collect. What is your favorite piece of art that you own?"

"For that you need to come into the bedroom with me."

Max gave her his best flirty grin. "Is that right?"

"Follow me, Mr. Max W."

Lydia wove him skillfully through her party, leaving Susannah behind. Lydia took him through the expansive living room into a wide, windowless, and dark-wood lined dining room covered in drawings, some of which Max also recognized—sketches by Robert Rauschenberg. At the swinging doors to the kitchen, they went right down a narrow hallway and then into a large bedroom, a canopied bed in the middle of it, the shades open to the falling snow over the park.

For a moment Max thought she was perhaps going to lift that billowy long white skirt of hers, some kind of play she made for younger men, as in *This is the only art you need to know*, but she said, "It's over here, above my bed."

As they both moved down the side of the bed to get a better look, Max saw a small painting of the sun, unadorned, floating big and yellow in a sea of a blue.

"I bought it for a dollar in a Tibetan market."

Max smiled at her as if this were the coolest thing, and not the cliché he considered it to be, the rich Western woman who could have any piece of art choosing this as her favorite. Behind it all was the statement of power, her telling Max that she alone got to decide what had value. She had taken this exact same walk many, many times, he knew, and had said these exact words to many others.

"I can see why you like it."

"Why's that?"

"The simplicity."

"Yes. You are right. Now come this way."

They headed toward the windows, across the bed, and Lydia stopped now in front of another painting, small and rectangular, almost entirely in blue, a woman standing against a wall.

"Now, this is my second-favorite painting." Lydia smiled.

Here again was the power, and the irony of it all, the contrast, for Max had studied enough to recognize the author's hand, a Picasso, Blue Period.

Lydia must have seen the look on his face, for she quickly said, "Would you like to be alone with it for a moment?"

"That's a terrible idea. I might slip it into my coat. I always secretly wanted to be an art thief."

Lydia laughed and he did, too, though Max was only partially joking. For if he thought he could have gotten it out of there and then found a way to move it, which given its profile would have been impossible, he might have considered it.

Instead Lydia led him back out to her party and left him after making introductions to a group from Egypt, of all places, who were academics from what Max could tell, critics, and they had a pleasant enough conversation, though while they talked, Max looked past them to where Susannah stood in a small group, staring at her until she felt the heat of his eyes and had no choice but to return his gaze, which she did with a wry, nervous smile.

In time Max headed to the bar for another drink. He stopped behind Susannah, and sensing his presence, she began to turn her head when he leaned down toward her, his breath on the back of her neck.

In a soft whisper, Max said, "Let's get out of here."

"I can't yet," she whispered back.

Forty minutes later they were on the elevator down to the lobby, then out into the snowy night.

"One drink at my place," Max had said, and she had said okay to this, telling him she couldn't be long, that she had a teenage son at home, something that normally was a deal breaker for him—no husbands, no wives, no kids, was his rule—but tonight he put it aside.

At the corner of Seventy-fourth, Max flagged down a cab, a luxury for him. He couldn't remember the last time he had been in a cab. They rode slowly in the dark down the snowy avenues, one third the length of the city to Alphabet City.

Max believed he had the gift to read people. He imagined he could often tell what they desired even before they knew it themselves. So when they came up the four flights of stairs to his studio apartment, one high-ceilinged room with books piled everywhere, some primitive paintings he had made on the walls, his bed a double mattress on the floor separated from the rest of the room by hanging tapestries, he led Susannah to the lone, visibly used low-slung midcentury couch and told her to wait there while he made them both a drink.

Max returned with a little of the only thing he had, some kind of dark rum, in small mason jars with single ice cubes. He handed hers to her.

"What is it?"

He told her. Before she could take so much as a sip, he said, "Take off your clothes."

She laughed. "Excuse me?"

"I want you to model for me."

"What makes you think I would do that?"

Everything about you, he wanted to say.

Some women want to be watched, to be gazed upon, and to have men drink them up with their eyes. She was one of them; Max saw it in her face. Her job now was to protest a bit before she relented.

"You have modeled before."

"Yes, but in college. That was forever ago."

"Well, then you know what to do."

"Yes, I should leave." She didn't move from her spot.

"But you don't want to."

"Tell me what the *W* is short for."

"Westmoreland."

"Why don't you use that?"

"Because my grandfather was a war criminal."

"Your grandfather?"

"General Westmoreland. He led the army in Vietnam."

"Nobody knows that."

"You'd be surprised."

"Okay."

"Can you take off your clothes, please?"

Susannah looked around the room. Max saw her mind whirring with the possibilities, weighing her options, the pitting of raw desire against practical concerns. She brought the rum to her lips and sipped its molasses sweetness, and he knew he had her. She wasn't going to leave; she was going to cross this divide with him.

"It's very bright in here. And I have mom tits."

"I don't care."

"Still, it's so bright."

"I have candles."

Max went to the cabinet above the sink and took out some beeswax candles he had left there, half-burned but in holders, and brought them out and placed them on the coffee table and lit them. He then dimmed the main light switch partway, enough that the candlelight now licked up the walls in hiccups toward the ceiling.

"Okay."

"I can't believe I am doing this." Susannah shook her head.

"Just a body. After all, what is the physical?"

"What are you going to do? Draw?"

"Take notes."

"Notes?"

"It's my process."

"It's like a nude beach."

"What do you mean?"

"I'm talking to myself," she said. "You just have to do it all at once."

She was magnificent. The way she stood, turning her back to him, reaching behind her to deftly unzip herself, the wriggling out of her red dress, the unsnapping of her bra, the sense of weight lifted, the pile of clothes on the floor, her panties the last, falling softly on the pile with a release of her fingers.

She turned back to Max, letting her arms fall to her side. He shamelessly took her in, as he knew she wanted him to. Her heavy breasts, the slope of her belly, the spiderweb of stretch marks above her narrow waist, the curve of her, the golden hue of her thighs.

"How do you want me?"

"Lie down please. Your head propped up on your elbow."

For the next forty-five minutes he moved around her with a pencil and a notepad, studying her as if she were a problem to be solved. He arranged her different ways. She gave in to it fully, as he suspected she might, since after all, hard as it might be to believe, this was more about her than it was about him.

What Max did with everything he learned—the strength of her, the fragility of her, the perfection, the flaws, all of it colluding as one to become the singular her, the singular Susannah—didn't matter so much as that she was the art, just as he thought of himself as the art.

Mostly what he did was write down phrases. *She stands feral like a deer. Eyes, wet, sad, hiding. She hates her nose and is wrong for hating it. Does she even know what love is? Scars profound and narrative, each tangled one of them.*

And so on.

The next day Max would take those phrases and put them all over a big, stretched-out canvas. He would adorn them with swirls of white and black paint so that the words floated in a sea of it. Poetry? Painting? Or was it the fraudulent bullshit of a man without much natural talent trying to make his way?

He would leave that to others to decide, but he thought that a life lived well had a lot in common with sleight of hand. Make them look one way, and they won't even know what it is they are seeing. They will believe you. The assumption is always to believe. When you got right down it, that was the only thing Max believed.

Eventually, that night, it was Susannah who came to him. He would remember the flush in her face when she rose off the couch, having had enough of his earnest attention. How she moved into him, lifting her head up to his, their lips colliding while his hand, on the small of her back, brought her closer. Max took her to bed.

They fucked slowly and patiently, gentle waves slapping on a beach. After, they lay together for a while in silence, and Max saw no darkness in her that first night, not even when they stood outside and said goodbye in the chill with the snow tumbling down. He saw only the light she had within her, bright as the moon, and he wanted to see her again. Only with time would he learn that we all have light, and we all have dark. Sometimes it's up to us which side wins. And sometimes it is not.

SUSANNAH'S BEST FRIEND FROM NEW YORK, Rose, used to repeat this joke about how women know if they are going to fuck a man as soon as they shake hands. Susannah always thought it was just that—a joke—until the night Max walked into Lydia's. He was gorgeous. Not in the usual ways either. He was tall and had a good jaw. But he was also bald or, at least, had shaved what might have been left. The day after, Susannah called Rose and said he was the Ed Harris bald-man exception, and everyone says that but in this case it was true.

It was something about his hands on hers. Susannah always loved a man's hands the most. His big hands felt electric. And then there was how he stared at her. She never felt more solid, less translucent, than when he looked at her.

She wasn't looking for a man. She had basically given up on that. People think New York must be easy for women—so many men! Men of all kinds and types, but more women than men are in New York. Susannah had been married for a long time. But then Joseph died and the idea of someone else was impossible to imagine. It took everything she had just to learn how to breathe again.

Susannah met Joseph when she was an art student at Pratt. Later, she would say he saved her life. She had been having panic attacks and didn't even know what they were. Sometimes she thought that her heart was going to explode in her chest: a bomb about to go off and the shrapnel like exploding stars destroying all of her. She was convinced she was going to die.

One night after she smoked a joint with friends, it came on like a storm. She snuck away by herself and walked to St. Vincent's Hospital, and the nurses left her in the waiting room for four hours, as if there was nothing wrong. Her heart was pounding out of her chest and she could not stop crying, but they did not care. From their perspective, Susannah was a twenty-one-year-old woman saying she was having a heart attack when she was probably just stoned.

Almost to placate her, she thought, they eventually brought her into a room and hooked her up to an EKG machine. The Indian doctor told her she was suffering from anxiety. He said, go home and get some sleep. And tomorrow go to the college health center and ask to see a therapist.

That is how Susannah met Joseph. He was her therapist. He was forty-nine years old, slightly heavy, and stood only five foot six. But he had a great head of curly dark hair gone to salt and pepper on the sides, intense black eyes, and he spoke with such assurance about everything. His voice was calming like a metronome. Susannah loved his voice and she loved how he used words. She couldn't get enough of his voice. Just the sound of it was enough for her to feel at ease, to stop being aware of her heart.

Others might have said that she fell under his spell. Some of her friends from that time went even further and suggested, though less directly to her, that he had exploited her; so typical, an older man in a professional role of authority taking advantage of a young woman. Rose, who was most direct with Susannah, even said that she worried that Susannah had Stockholm syndrome, where the kidnap victim falls in love with her captor.

Susannah would have said those points of view insulted her role in how things evolved, for she made the first move. She was the one who persuaded Joseph to ignore his ethical obligations. Later, he would say he didn't have a choice. Susannah had seduced him.

How could he have possibly said no? You might be able to say no to beauty once, Joseph said, but you cannot say no to it the second time.

She had been in therapy with him for a month, twice-weekly sessions that she looked forward to more than anything else in her life then. He was teaching her how to live. Susannah gave herself over completely to his soothing voice, his calibrated words, and after their first session she told herself that she would do whatever he asked.

She hungered for his attention. She hated how fast that fifty-five minutes went, and she would often stare over his shoulder at the clock on the bookcase, trying to will it to slow down. *Just let me be here longer, please.*

One night after one of these sessions, Susannah walked out into the spring night and waited across Fourth Street from his office. She wasn't positive—he was secretive about these things—but she thought she was his last patient of the day. She stood there for about fifteen minutes, then he came out the door, shuffling with that odd walk of his. He didn't look across the street but instead headed right, and she followed him from the other side. He didn't go far. Halfway down the block he stopped and went into the Slaughtered Lamb Pub.

In her head, Susannah counted to fifty. When she reached it, she crossed the street and went to the door of the bar and opened it. The small wooden tables inside were half-full and so was the bar, with Joseph sitting by himself partway down, reading a tattered paperback with a tumbler of brown liquor in front of him. He bent forward as he read, getting close to the page, as if the reading glasses on the end of his nose didn't quite work. With time she would find this habit of his endearing.

So engrossed was he in the book that he didn't look up as she slid onto the stool next to him, tight enough that he had to shuffle a bit to his left to let her in, which he did without glancing in her direction.

Once she sat, Susannah turned and studied his oblivious face for a moment. His gaze didn't waver from his book, and she could see the little tufts of gray hair in his ears. She was so close to him that she could have just leaned forward and kissed the smooth flesh of his cheeks, the place where the lines were starting to frame his mouth. She could smell his aftershave, like mint.

Then the bartender was in front of her. "Something to drink?"

"I'll have what he's having." She pointed to the tumbler in front of Joseph.

"Jack neat," the bartender said.

"Susannah," Joseph said, her voice getting his attention. "What are you doing here?"

She turned fully to him now, and he glared at her. "Hi, Joseph."

"You can't be here."

She looked around in mock surprise. "Why not? It's a public place, isn't it?"

"We talked about this when I began seeing you. I gave you my rules on if we see each other in public. There are ethical obligations. We are not friends. We cannot be friends."

"I don't want to be your friend, Joseph."

He gave her that famous hard stare of his, one she had seen before, over the glasses perched on his nose, as if, should he glare at her, she would just suddenly bend to his will, stand up, throw a ten on the bar for her untouched drink, and walk out into the spring evening.

But something else was in that look because she had seen it before from him, how he took her in sometimes with his eyes when he thought she didn't notice.

She didn't budge, and Joseph turned back to his book and pretended she wasn't there. They sat in relative silence, the bar conversations and hum of the restaurant around them. Susannah liked just being close to him like this, as if she could hear him thinking, that deep, delicate mind whirring like a clock.

When he finished his drink, Susannah thought he would pay and leave, but he ordered another, and she did, too, and when he took a pull off his whiskey, he looked at her and Susannah boldly said, "Take me home with you."

"That's not a good idea."

"There are other therapists. I can see someone else."

"That's hardly the point."

"Take me home with you."

That night in his book-lined West Village loft, he screwed her the way she imagined only an older man could. He was not like the college boys she had been with before, who treated sex like some kind of sport or a race, climbing on her like a rabbit and just going.

Instead he undressed her, savored her, talked to her in that deep, soothing voice, and loved her slowly and beautifully. Afterward, they lay in his big bed with the windows open to the blare of the city, Joseph on his back breathing hard, her right hand running over his hairy broad chest as she dove her face into the crook of his arm and smelled his tired body.

A week later Susannah left her high-rise dorm and moved in with him. Once a week she visited his office as she had before, and they pretended they were not lovers, that they did not live together, that she did not want to be his wife.

For those fifty-five minutes he was her therapist, and he challenged her, and sometimes she pushed back. But their life at home always seeped in and it was different. Most important to Susannah, though, her panic receded. When she was with Joseph, it always did, as if he were some giant placebo she popped into her mouth. Just hearing his voice calmed her, and in those early years together he owned her completely. One moment Susannah was all wild pony, and the next she was channeling the passive compliance of her Spanish mother, and Joseph knew how to get her there.

He saw right through her. One time they were in session, early summer, and they had been living together for a few months. Outside the windows of his office it was pouring hard, a late-afternoon thunderstorm and dark like winter. Susannah had been talking about her parents, how they didn't understand why she would want to go to art school, why anyone would even think that becoming a painter was an option.

Her parents were immigrants who left Madrid when she was six and her sister was eight and brought them to Queens for a job where her dad drove a delivery truck. Her parents were deeply Catholic, and all through high school not a single boy had ever made it past the doorway of their small house. Her mother went to Mass every single morning. Her father went on both weekend mornings.

Susannah knew the things they hoped for her, and none of them involved whom she quickly became, the girl who in high school smoked pot and hung out with black boys with dreadlocks. She was the girl who only wanted to draw things, not study. She found everything else boring and distracting. She embodied everything her parents feared about coming to America.

Why couldn't she be more like her big sister, Cristina, who studied accounting and had already found a good man, a fellow Spanish

striver named David who had his eyes on Wall Street and doing something with his life? On making a family? How could she tell her
parents that what they had, the life, the beliefs, the closed tiny world,
was exactly what she was running from? That she only believed in
Jesus on Sundays and then only for a moment, when Susannah found
herself staring at him suspended above the altar and something about
the sadness in his downward-turned face on the cross spoke to her,
not as God but as a sad-eyed man?

A few weeks before, Cristina had come to visit her in the city. She
had made the mistake of telling her about Joseph, for Susannah loved
him and wanted her sister to know, and even though she saw in Cristina's face the sharp look of disapproval, she pressed forward. That
night, after Cristina left, Susannah's father called her.

"End it," he said in Spanish, "Or don't come back here."

"I love him."

"End it or don't come back, Susannah."

"You should meet him, Papa."

"The man is my age. You are a child. It is sick and wrong. End it,
Susannah." He hung up.

Sitting in Joseph's office later, they were talking about this, and
suddenly Joseph's eyes narrowed and he gave her that look, the ques-
tioning one he had.

"You are taking your birth control?"

"What kind of question is that? Of course I am."

"I haven't seen you take it."

"What the fuck are you saying? That I am trying to get pregnant?"

Joseph shrugged, as if this were no big deal. "Some women do
it, you know. They do it to accelerate things, to make them more
serious. I want you to know I would be very upset, Susannah."

She started to cry, more in anger than in sadness. She rose out of her chair. "Is this what you think of me? Is this really who you think I am?"

"Sit down."

"Don't you tell me what to fucking do."

She left, out into his waiting room, down the rickety wooden stairs, and through the door to Fourth Street and the falling rain.

ANOTHER TIME JOSEPH GAVE HER a bunch of tests, to establish a baseline, he said, including one, a questionnaire, he called "the 'fuck you' test." The higher you scored on it, the less likely you were to say "fuck you," or so he said. It had a more technical name but she didn't remember what it was. It measured both conformity and leadership, she remembered. On conformity she scored only 2 percent on a scale of 100, which meant she was very likely to say "fuck you," and he should have known that, she thought, and that what followed was his fault.

After that afternoon fight in his office, he wanted to watch her take her birth control at night, and he was vigilant about it. Each night before bed he waited for Susannah to slip that small white pill on her tongue and swallow it, looking at her with some kind of paternalistic pride, in her view, as if she were a child.

That look of smug self-satisfaction on his face made her pretend a month later she had her period, and instead of the white pills, one day after another she took the little red ones instead, the fake ones you popped just to stay in the routine.

During that time and on those summer nights with the sounds of the city filling her ears, Susannah rode Joseph as if it were her job.

And that was the thing about it. She was only twenty-one, and with all the wisdom of that age she wasn't thinking about a baby, or a life, but only about getting pregnant. It wasn't conscious, this act, and as impossible as that sounds, it was simply about not wanting Joseph, or anyone else, telling her what to do. Susannah couldn't abide that, which was why she went to art school in the first place and why she graded high on the "fuck you" test.

She knew she was pregnant long before she confirmed it, and long before she told Joseph. Susannah felt that baby growing in her like a plant. It reminded her of when she was a kid and her father would tell her not to eat watermelon seeds, that if she did, inside her belly a watermelon would grow and take over her whole insides, leaves growing up toward her mouth. Susannah used to believe that, and sometimes in the bedroom she shared with Cristina, Susannah would lie under the covers at night and imagine what that would feel like. Her father said it to make her laugh or maybe to scare her, but it did neither. Susannah loved the idea that she could make fruit.

For sixteen weeks she harbored this secret. Her belly rounded out, her breasts got bigger and sensitive, and Joseph didn't notice at all. He did notice that a calm had come over her, as if the fire and the anger she had carried like a cross had somehow been—*extinguished* is the wrong word—turned into love.

Susannah loved Joseph more and took care of him, and he in turn began to show her a kindness that went beyond his interest in her body and dissecting her mind. Some mornings those days before his first appointment they would lie in bed for hours, both awake, curled into each other like sleeping puppies.

Then she told him.

His fury showed in his balled-up fists and the vein prominent on his forehead, and for a moment she thought he might strike her.

"Abort it."

She shook her head. "I won't. I am Catholic."

He laughed at this. "Catholic? Oh, come on. Being raised Catholic doesn't make you Catholic. We're not having a baby."

"You're right. *We* are not. *I* am."

In that moment, she saw something that she had not previously known to be true. Joseph needed her as much as she needed him. All along, she had felt as if he owned all the power, that she lived in his place, not theirs; that he was healing her, and not her, him. But in truth, he didn't want to lose her. He couldn't imagine losing her. Susannah found something sad in seeing this in him, all his supremacy fading from his knowing black eyes and leaving a paunchy middle-aged man in its place.

A healthy big baby boy with a thatch of black hair and dark Spanish eyes came that following February. She named him Ferdinand, after her favorite children's book, about the bull that doesn't want to fight and only wants to smell the flowers. She named him Ferdinand but she called him Freddy, and she realized that while she thought she had been in love before she had a baby, she had not. Not even close.

Susannah was entirely unprepared for what she felt. In Freddy's first months, sometimes it overwhelmed her and she couldn't stop crying. For all his years of listening in treatments, Joseph had no way of understanding why she was inconsolable, for it was definitely closer to joy than sadness, but somewhere in the ambiguous middle between those poles.

On Easter Sunday of that year she bundled up Ferdinand and took him in a cab out to Queens. It was the end of March and the day was sunny but unseasonably cold. Her family didn't know she was coming. When the cab went over the bridge from Manhattan, the East River gray below them, she looked out the window to the small web of neighborhoods, tiny houses upon tiny houses, where her family had moved to from Spain when she was child.

Susannah had the cab drop her off a few houses away from the small ranch house that her parents owned. She wore a scarf covering her hair, a bright red one, and a long overcoat, and cradled Ferdinand in her arms, his tiny body within the warmth of her coat. He had fallen asleep on the ride and was just waking up, beautiful and sleepy eyed and not yet asking for milk.

When she reached the front of the house, she stopped for a moment. She knew that with the scarf on her head she was virtually unrecognizable. Even though the day was bright and sunny, her parents' house was on the shady side of the street, and through the picture window she saw her sister, Cristina, in front of the dining room table, setting it for dinner. Behind her was her husband, David, holding their toddler, Susannah's nephew, Jorge, whom she had never met. Her father, short and stout with his head of thick gray hair, was tousling the boy's hair. Her mother, as usual, was invisible, no doubt in the kitchen, tending to a roast leg of lamb, her potatoes, stained red with paprika, in a cast-iron pan on the stovetop.

Susannah walked up the driveway. Up the cement path to the metal screen door, the same one that had always been there, a giant X over the faded glass, the one that slammed shut when it closed. Behind it the storm door was a solid pale yellow, no windows. She looked at the glowing orange circle around the doorbell, then down at Ferdinand, his big dark eyes open and wet and looking back at her. Then she rang the doorbell.

She heard footfalls. The door swung open and it was Cristina, and Susannah watched her face go strange when she saw the son in Susannah's arms.

"Susannah. What?"

But before Susannah could answer, her father was there, shorter than her sister, his shirt with his name on it, his thick gray hair pushed off to the right side, and his wrinkled olive face. He looked from Susannah's face down to Ferdinand.

"Papa," Susannah said. "This is your grandson."

"That's not my grandson," he spat back.

"He came out of my body."

Her father shook his head. His eyes were dark. "Not in my house, Susannah. You are not welcome here."

She began to cry, and her sister, now behind her father, did as well. Her father loved children and Susannah did not expect this cruelty. Behind them Susannah saw her small mother in her apron, and despite the wanting and the sadness in her eyes, Susannah knew her mother was no help at all. Her mother didn't even bother to move forward.

"Papa, we're here for Easter."

He closed the door and she heard the turn of the lock, and on cue Freddy started to scream. Her baby was hungry.

They moved away from the house and to the curb, where she sat down and in the cold day opened her coat and unbuttoned her blouse to give her son a nipple. She felt the release into his mouth like a shudder. She leaned her face down into his wet black hair while he sucked and she wiped her tears on his tiny head.

They were in New York City, on a neighborhood street, one of the most densely populated places on earth. In the distance she heard the rumble of cars on the expressway somewhere above them. But the street itself was holiday quiet. Everyone was inside. Behind them stood her childhood home. In front, across the river, lay Manhattan. In six years Joseph would die of a heart attack, making Susannah a widow at twenty-seven. But in that moment watching her baby nurse, she decided that the world would always be just the two of them, her and Freddy, and that was okay. What else did they need?

Thirteen years later, Max walked into a party.

MAX WAS ABOUT TO GO onstage in Chicago when Susannah called to tell him about the note. He stood next to this graduate student from the Art Institute watching the big theater-style space slowly fill up. She was a pretty brunette who had been assigned as his handler and who had, the night before at the dinner the faculty threw for him at the chair's house, made it abundantly clear without saying anything that if he wanted to take her back to his hotel, she would be more than willing to open her legs. When he was younger, Max might have taken her up on it, but one of the greatest gifts of getting older, he thought, was learning discipline. Deferring gratification can be a pleasure unto itself.

His phone started to vibrate in his pocket, and when he pulled it out, it was Susannah. He declined the call, and a moment later it rang again. They had an agreement that if either of them needed to reach the other one urgently, they would call twice in rapid succession. That said, the only time they had ever used this was during a fight, when one of them disappeared to cool off. It wasn't really the intent, but they did it anyway. *No one ignored a Bat-Signal*, Max thought. But now, as far as he knew, they weren't fighting, so he answered.

"Hey, baby, I'm about to go on. All okay?"

Her words came out in a torrent. A blur of nonsense at first, something about running in the rain, and Max thought, *She is having one of her bouts and I can't deal with this now*. He needed to have his head in the right space. The stage was in front of him, only a few feet away, waiting for him, the place he belonged more than any other. Then Susannah was talking about some note, and when she read what it said, she suddenly had his attention.

"Should I call the police?" she said, almost pleading, wanting Max to solve it for her, to fulfill her need for everything to have an easy solution, a pill you could take to make it go away.

"Wait, wait. What did it say again?"

She told him: "'I know who you are.'"

"No. Don't call anyone, okay? It's nothing, really. I'm sure of it. Listen, I've got to go, honey. And I'll be home tonight and we can talk?"

"Okay, Max," she said, her voice suddenly frail.

He hung up and slid the phone back into his pocket. He turned to the student in front of him. "Sorry about that."

A moment later, the faculty chair of the art program was next to him, a slender young Malaysian woman named Li. "Ready, Max?"

"Always," he said with a thin smile, though he didn't believe it anymore.

"Great." She bounded onstage, and her introduction came to him in pieces: Max W was one of the significant voices in art today, and he was transforming the very understanding of what it meant to be a cultural producer. His work had been . . .

Then Max walked slowly up the stairs to the wide stage, stopping to hug Li, taking her tiny body in his arms for a moment as if they knew each other better than they did, even though he had only met her for the first time last night. It was all part of the theater. The applause washed over him like warm rain. Max went to the podium and removed the microphone from its stand and looked out to the sea of faces. He waited for the silence, and a moment later it came. The room went still. He stared out at them and he didn't speak right away. This was the moment he loved, playing with the audience, the tease of knowing they wanted to hear his voice and he was going to make them wait.

But today something else was at work. Those words that Susannah had told him over the phone were burrowing like a worm into his mind. Max saw them floating in the air in front of him.

I know who you are.

Someone was fucking with him, and he was going to find out who. But first he had to get through this talk. *Okay,* he told himself, *energy. Bring the energy.*

Max walked to the middle of the stage and stopped. He smiled broadly. "You are the art. We are the art. Everything you have ever learned is total bullshit. Listen. Listen to my story. Listen to the story I am about to tell you."

He felt the warm embrace of hundreds of people leaning into his words. He allowed it to engulf him for a moment, a summer breeze pushing him back, and then he leaned back into them.

ON THE FLIGHT HOME MAX sipped vodka on ice and looked out the window at the thick dark clouds. He was new to academia, but eight months was plenty of time to see it was a thicket of petty jealousies and politics, tiny turf battles over things of insignificance. And nothing was worse than being popular and current, especially among an aging faculty. Max knew his hiring was controversial. Breaking new ground will always piss off the status quo.

But why leave a note? If someone were on to him, wouldn't the person just go to the chair of the department or even the provost of the university and say, *This is what I found out*? The university would have no choice but to fire Max. Though the appointment was just one piece of the puzzle—the talks and the word paintings were far more lucrative—it was the foundation, the agency Max needed to be Max W. It conferred legitimacy on the entire enterprise. If it went away, everything he had worked to create would unravel. And if someone had really started to dig, well, then, it would all be over.

MAX THOUGHT SOMETIMES THAT IT was all as simple as his having been born wrong. He was born into the wrong family, into the wrong name, and into the wrong identity. He didn't become a fraud, in his view, but emerged into the world that way fully formed.

He was born Phil Wilbur in the tiny western New York town of Interlaken, located between two Finger Lakes, Seneca and Cayuga, a sad little town full of broken people that once he left he never returned to.

His mother, Debbie, had him when she was sixteen, which Max always joked was a clear formula for success. They moved nearly every two years when he was young, but all within the same five-mile stretch of rural highway running between the lakes and through the woods. He was not sure why they moved so much, since each place was the same, some shitty apartment in a drafty old farmhouse.

Sometimes his mother worked as a waitress and sometimes she cleaned houses, but mostly she drank cheap beer and chain-smoked generic cigarettes and wore pancake-thick blue eye shadow and got sucked into fucked-up relationships with a parade of losers that began, Max guessed, with his dad—whom she pointed out once at the grocery store a couple of weeks before he went to prison for kicking a guy to death outside a bar in Seneca Falls.

Max's father knew he was looking at his son, but he didn't come over and say hello. He looked right through the two of them. The only thing he ever gave Max was his name, which, when Max grew old enough, he didn't want anyway. Because of this history, when he looked back on it, Max felt as if he had grown up not belonging to anyone or anything, so that when it became time, it was easier to leave.

One day in the summer Max was sixteen, he and his only close friend, Todd, hitchhiked down the highway to Ithaca. Todd knew a guy down there who sold pot, and the goal was to hitchhike there, score a bag of weed, then spend the day walking around the small city streets looking for girls.

As it turned out, Todd's friend didn't have any to sell, but he got them high and they walked around anyway. Down near the bus station was a group of kids around their age, smoking cigarettes, sitting out front with guitars and signs asking for money, and Todd asked them if they had any green to sell. While they didn't, that got them into conversation, and Todd and Max ended up spending the day with them, passing flasklike bottles of hobo wine. They were travelers. Crusty punks they called themselves, and when they told Max what they did, move from friendly city to friendly city, warm places in winter, up north in summer, camping where they could, scrapping together money and sharing everything, Max thought it was the most romantic and awesome thing he had ever heard. It beat the shit out of living in a crappy apartment with his mom, who was never around anyway.

So that night both Max and Todd packed up backpacks, and the next night they slept out under the stars near the railroad tracks and got good and drunk with their new friends. For the next three years, Max traveled with them. They went as far south as Tallahassee, and as far north as Burlington, Vermont, where many years later Max and Susannah and Freddy would make their home.

The punks lived on the streets and got hassled by the cops and became pros at all kinds of things. Each of the travelers had skills, and Max's skill was with words. From an early age, he could talk someone into practically anything if he tried hard enough. He was especially good at panhandling. People trusted his face.

But then one night, in New York City, Max had an awakening. He was about to turn twenty years old, and suddenly the life had lost its appeal. He was tired of being high and he was tired of being hungry and he was tired of fucking in tents where everyone around him could hear. This whole idea of being outside it all, something they talked about all the time with deep pride, how the rest of the world was straight and they were bent, all these sheep moving in a herd down city streets and these travelers doing their own thing, man, suddenly turned for him.

Max didn't want to be outside it all. He wanted to be inside it and he wanted to stir it all up. He wanted to figure out how it worked and make it his own.

This part of the story had become part of his mythology. It was always in his talk. What happened next, though, was certainly not.

Max with a group of four others had slept that night against a fence in a part of the Hudson Yards where they were starting to build a high-rise. The river was right behind it, and they stayed up talking and drinking and watching the boat traffic, like rich people with a view. Around them was a construction site, and it was a pretty good place to sleep if they didn't mind waking with the sun and before the crews arrived. Though sometimes, such as on this night, they got chased away in the middle of the night by a security truck and scattered quickly, gathering their stuff and running toward the West Side Highway. Usually they would find each other, regroup, and find another place to bed.

But tonight, for some reason, Max just kept running. He ran up the side of the highway until his lungs started to burn. His friends, including the girl Hannah, this slender wisp of a thing he had been sleeping with for about a month, were somewhere behind him. For once he didn't care.

He walked until dawn. There is no trudge like a highway trudge, and by the time the sun came up, Max was on the side of 95 North with his thumb out. It was late June, and the sun even at this time of morning was hot. Cars and eighteen-wheelers were streaming by him, the hard rattle of them, and no one cared about this kid on the highway with a heavy backpack, since nothing says distress more than having your entire life in a bag.

But then a black open Jeep Wrangler pulled over into the breakdown lane in front of him, and Max ran up on it.

Behind the wheel was a man a little older than himself. He looked like Max actually, though his eyes were brown and he was almost as pretty as a girl, with long lashes and smooth cheeks and closely cropped hair.

"Where you headed?"

"Anywhere north."

"Hop in."

The air was thick and warm as they drove, and with the sides of the Jeep open the heavy weight of the heat smacked Max in the face.

"Hey." The guy driving turned to Max, speaking with a drawl that he would later learn was South Carolina Lowcountry. "I'm Max W."

"Phil Wilbur."

"Phil, a pleasure."

"Just *W*?"

"Yes, sir. I'm from Charleston, and my last name, which is Westmoreland, is a big deal down there. The Westmorelands in

Charleston are like the first military family. Fucking royalty. Have you heard of General Westmoreland?"

Max shook his head. "No."

"Well, he ran Vietnam. The war. You heard of Vietnam?"

"Yes."

"Well, he ran that shit. Some people think he's a war criminal. Though not in Charleston. He's a fucking god there. And he was also my grandfather. But since I don't think killing lots of people is something to be proud of, and if you didn't notice, I'm also gayer than a picnic basket, I decided I would just call myself Max W. Plus, it sounds cool, don't you think?"

Max looked at him. His pretty brown eyes, the way his whole face seemed to laugh when he smiled. "Sure."

"Where you going, Phil?"

"I don't know."

"Well, all right, then. Maybe we just drive then? What do you say?"

"Sounds good to me." Shortly after that, Max fell asleep.

When he woke, they were near Albany, New York. He must have been asleep for at least three hours.

"I thought about waking you," Max W said, "but you were snoring like a bear, man. Thought you needed your rest. But hope I didn't pass your stop."

"I don't have a stop. I'm just traveling."

"Yeah? Well, if you want, you can come up with me. Going to my grandfather's camp in the Adirondacks for a few nights. Place is empty. My family is usually there only in August. Needed to get out of Dodge, you know?"

Max looked at him, his nice smile. "Yeah?"

"Yeah, man, definitely."

"All right." Max sank back into his seat.

An hour and a half later they pulled into the most remarkable driveway—if you can call it that—he had ever seen. It was a path through the woods, off the rural highway in Keene, New York, and at first it meandered in a single lane through trees, until it began to climb sharply. An ancient guardrail on the left looked as if it was made of cast iron, and as they went up, the drop-off on that side got steeper and steeper, and to the right of them the hill climbed upward in a forest of spruce and birch.

"We climbing a mountain?"

"Fuck yeah," Max W said. "The camp is at the top of the mountain."

"Crazy."

Max wasn't sure what he expected, a cabin maybe, but certainly not the house that greeted them at the end of that winding road. Built on a gentle knoll at the top, the sprawling old dark green wooden house had a giant porch that wrapped around it, full of chairs everywhere, a porch that looked as if it could seat well over a hundred. After they parked, Max turned around, and below them he could see a massive expanse of valley, and all around higher mountains loomed over. Looking down the valley, he felt as if he could see a hundred miles in the distance.

Inside were thirty-foot ceilings, walls and ceilings paneled with dark brown wood, deer heads on the wall, ornate woodwork, a massive curved staircase, and a fireplace that he could have walked into and stood in.

"You're rich, huh?"

"My great-grandfather on my mother's side was a famous artist. Funny, right? War criminal on my father's side, artist on my mom's. Who do you think I take after? Hudson River School, he was. Heard of it? Lots of famous painters. He built this place in the 1890s. My family has been coming here every summer since."

"I'd live here all the time."

Max W laughed. "The only heat is that fireplace. And there's no insulation. Plus, you could never get up the road."

"Got any booze?"

"Tons. Come on."

In the big dining room with a chandelier made out of antlers was an old giant hutch, and inside it was a liquor cabinet with dozens upon dozens of bottles of all kinds of things, some of them covered in dust a half inch thick. Max W grabbed a bottle of bourbon, and they went out to the porch with two small glasses, and sitting there, with the long corridor of the valley beneath them, no houses visible, and just the two of them alone on top of a mountain getting drunk, Max suddenly felt the world was vast.

Max W did most of the talking. He told his story. Like his great-grandfather, he was an artist, too, he said. He had gone to this fancy art school in California to paint and then also did graduate school there. "I got an MFA," he said with a smile, "which makes me a Master of Fine Fucking Arts."

His trust fund allowed him to live in New York in a small apartment and try to crack the art world, as he put it. But lately he had been having doubts about all of it.

"So much bullshit, Phil, you wouldn't believe it. The whole gallery system is fucked. It ain't who you know, it's who you blow, you know what I mean?"

Max nodded as if he did, but these were all new words to him.

"Not sure I even want to paint anymore."

"Why not?"

"'Cause talent doesn't matter, man. You see who gets rich and famous, right? It's never about the art. Well, usually not. It's who can spin a tale about their art. It's just fucked up, I tell you."

Max found himself considering this, the idea that talent didn't matter, because he didn't have any. Later he would consider this more, when the idea of becoming an artist himself would start to take hold of him, like a cold that turns into a virus.

But he wasn't there yet. Instead he looked out at the mountains next to this guy he had just met and watched the sun fade from the sky.

That night they grilled up a bunch of venison from the freezer that they thawed and opened and ate some cans of baked beans, too. The meat was especially good, and Max couldn't remember the last time he had eaten meat that tasted like that, if ever.

Max W showed him the house, and the art that had made his great-grandfather famous, some of which hung on those tall wooden walls. He showed him the eight bedrooms, and for the first time in his life Max wondered what it might be like to be rich, to have something like this.

He could also tell that Max W wanted to fuck him and was warming to different thoughts on how to present the idea. Max wasn't going to make it easy for him. Max knew all along that was the score, within minutes of getting in the car, but life on the road had taught him that both boys and girls wanted him, something about the energy he gave off, but he also had learned from experience how to defend against it.

After dinner they sat back out on the big porch next to each other on this long green bench and stared into the dark and smoked a joint. They had big glasses of bourbon and they had finished half of one open fifth and were on a new bottle. They grew quiet after the joint, and for Max this just amplified all the night sounds on the mountain, the shrill cry of coyotes far away, and closer, and more disconcertingly, some kind of grunting that sounded as if it was in the woods right below them. In his mind he pictured some big black bear moving through those trees in the dark, lumbering uphill, before rising up over the porch railing, big head and claws coming toward them.

"Any bears here?"

"Just you," Max W said, leaning in toward him now. This was the moment. Max looked straight ahead and felt him, his lips grazing Max's cheek and he turned toward him and allowed him to kiss him for the briefest of moments, turning away when he tried to put his tongue in Max's mouth.

Max reached down and unzipped his pants and pushed him that way. "That's all you get."

Max W slid down there and looked up at Max. "Well, that's an awful lot, Phil."

THERE WAS NO SPECIFIC MOMENT that Max could recall when he decided to kill him. It wasn't that night, letting him blow him was the least he could do. And it had nothing to do with his being gay—Max couldn't have cared less about that. It was just that the more they talked, this small germ of an idea Max had during the middle of that blow job—that he could kill him right now and not a soul would know Max was ever there—began to creep into his mind and it wouldn't let go.

Max said he wanted his own room, and Max W showed him to this room upstairs with a big canopied bed and Max said, "I'm serious. No coming in here, tonight, okay?"

"What part of Southern gentleman wasn't I clear about?"

Max smiled. "Okay."

He couldn't remember the last time he had slept in a real bed. It highlighted to him how much his whole body ached from years of sleeping outside. He sank into the soft mattress and in moments he was out.

When he woke, the sun was high in the sky and beaming in, the room stifling and smelling like old people. His room had its own bathroom—all the bedrooms did—and he stumbled in there and turned on the shower and kept the water cold and got under there and it felt like being reborn, all that water just pouring on him and wiping away whatever he had done the night before, whatever he had done for years now.

When Max went downstairs, Max W had made coffee and was about to cook omelets for the two of them, as if they were a regular old couple all of a sudden.

They spent the rest of that day fucking around. They climbed a little bit in the woods to see this view, the whole mountain range and, in the distance, Lake Champlain and on the other side Vermont. They nibbled on all kinds of food they found in the house, a bag of spicy venison jerky, and some chips that were sort of stale but still okay. They started drinking early because when it's just two guys alone on a mountain and they don't want to go anywhere, what else do they do?

Max W made a case to go into town, maybe go to the one bar down there, but Max discouraged him. Max had decided he didn't want anyone seeing both of them together.

"Man, why?" he said. "We got everything we need up here."

So instead they made gin and tonics and sat on that giant porch and watched the sun slowly fall behind the hills. For dinner they grilled a saddle of lamb, something Max had never heard of but it was a huge hunk of meat, and they ate that with frozen peas they cooked in butter and some potatoes they threw in a hobo pack on the grill, which was Max's contribution. A little road knowledge, he said.

Max W opened a dusty old bottle of red wine, which was kind of sour and colored brown, and later Max wished he had paid more attention to what it was, for while he certainly couldn't appreciate it then, it was probably some rare French vintage that he could have been conversant in, could reference at an opening or a cocktail party.

The meal was memorable. Max could still remember the taste of that tender lamb when it was pulled away from the bone, the smell of the fat. After eating, they sat happy and full and watched the dark gather.

They were next to each other in Adirondack chairs that were painted a deep dark green. The wine gave way to bourbon and Max W was getting drunk, and when he got drunk, his Southern accent went through the roof and he started to pontificate, picking up on the conversation they had had earlier about the whole art-world thing, and none of it made sense to Max and he wished Max W would quit it and let Max stare out into the dark and taste the smooth whiskey.

Later, he would also remember the glass in his hand, a big old-fashioned tumbler, leaded glass, heavy. He would remember the fractured sky, the place between day and night, the buzzing in his head from the whiskey. He saw the way Max W looked at him in the half dark from a foot away, how his face floated there in the air, big and fat like a peach.

What Max would never remember, though, was the whip slap of his arm, fast fast fast, or why he did it when he did, it was one of those things that just happened, instinct, id and fury taking over.

In front of him, Max W's face exploded as the glass hit it full on. It contorted sideways, mashing into itself and then releasing back to its full size. A half second later the blood was everywhere. The noise that came out of his mouth was terrifying. Max knew he had no choice but to finish what he had started then, which he did on that porch, and it didn't matter that Max W screamed for there was no one for miles to hear him. Then he was silent, for every act of violence eventually leads to silence.

Max was spent. He stumbled back into the big house and up those winding stairs and found his room from the night before and went into it and took off his stained clothes and collapsed onto the big canopied bed.

THE NEXT MORNING THE SKY was gray out the windows and Max's head ached from the booze, but he knew he had to reckon with a world of responsibility in that house. Max took the tablecloth off the huge dining-room table and he brought it out to the porch and he wrapped the body in it, which is how he thought of Max W now. He didn't want to have to look at him. So he dragged him to the edge of the porch and left him there while he cleaned.

He used towels on the big stuff and these he threw into the tablecloth with Max W. Then he used a spray bottle he found under the sink and paper towels and did his best to get everything up. He went around to every place in the house he could remember touching and he sprayed it down and wiped and scrubbed.

Max decided to hike down and away from the house, where the land was steep and harder to access. It would be easier to move the body downhill, and since it was so pitched, someone walking was less likely to come upon him.

He took a shovel he found in the garage and he needed to get as far away from the house as possible, but he also knew that when he returned to the site he would be dragging 150 pounds of dead weight awkwardly behind him.

He picked a spot on the side of that mountain overgrown with moss between two spruce trees, and the forest floor was wet and the earth moved easily with each dig of the shovel. The mosquitoes were everywhere, though, in his hair, on his neck, and he felt them biting and huge, and while he swiped at them when he could, mostly he just worked through it, like some kind of penance. Soon he had a hole about three feet deep, and six feet long. He returned up the hill to the house.

It took over two hours to get the bundle containing Max W down to the hole he had dug. He was too heavy to carry, so he dragged him like Santa Claus with a sack of toys as in some cartoon Max had seen when he was a kid.

He dragged him through heavy brush and then downhill through trees and over stumps and by the time he got him down there it felt as if his arms were about to fall off. Max stood breathing heavy and looking at this pile that barely fit into the ground. It occurred to him that he should put all of Max W's other stuff in there, too, his bag and his clothes and everything he had brought to the house with him. So before he filled in around Max W, he once again returned to the house.

Max W's backpack was in the kitchen where he'd left it. In there, in addition to his clothes, was a passport and a Dopp kit, which contained a barber's clippers, the secret to how he kept his head so closely shaved.

Mac took this out and went and looked at himself in the mirror. His hair, though already thinning in the front, was long and ragged and in places had rope-thick dreadlocks that hung down the sides of his head. He turned the clippers on to see if the batteries were charged and it came to life. He smiled into the mirror, though he couldn't do this here. He couldn't leave the hair with the DNA it would provide, and he couldn't leave it anywhere near the house.

In one of the bedrooms Max found a small antique round mirror on a stand and he took it and the clippers and went outside. This time, instead of hiking down the hill toward the new grave, he went up this scraggly hillside where the mountain continued. It was full of brush and slow going, but soon he found himself deep in the forest with the house far below.

Max stopped in front of a rocky outcropping and balanced the mirror on top of it and looked at himself. He turned on the clippers and went to work.

On the forest floor below, three years of his hair, three years of living on streets up and down the East Coast, fell onto old leaves and blended in.

In the mirror, Max barely recognized the man staring back at him, his whole life cut away in seconds, and here he was, brand-new.

He came back down the hill toward the house. As he was about to walk the final fifteen feet to the front porch, he heard the car before he saw it, parked in front with the engine running. Max was about to dive back into the woods but it was too late.

The car, red and white with a light rack on top and the word SHERIFF emblazoned on the side, was facing where he stood some twenty yards away, and anyone inside could easily have seen him.

Max dropped the mirror and the clippers on the ground and took the last step out of the break of trees onto the scraggly lawn that led to the house. He looked at the car and wondered how this might go down. He wondered if he might have the opportunity to fight or to flee, or if he would get shot.

The car door opened and a uniformed older man with a mustache got out and stood with the door cracked and gave him a wave that seemed entirely friendly.

"Hey, Max," he called.

Max realized that with his newly shaved head and from a distance he looked like Max W. People see what they expect to see, and given the context, of course the sheriff thought he was Max W.

"Hey," he shouted back, trying to sound like Max W, faking a Southern lilt, but didn't move any closer.

"Heard there was someone up here, just wanted to make sure it was one of you all."

"Thanks." Max waved again, as if to say *Dismissed*.

"Were you hiking?"

Max realized that fresh haircut aside, he must look rough and dirty, and he had to have blood on his clothes. "Oh, yeah."

"Well, all right then, be well."

Max waved as the sheriff backed his cruiser out and turned it around and went back down the narrow drive.

Max went to work fast. He was hungry as hell but food could wait. He had been hungrier. He took all of Max W's clothes and his bag and brought them down to the hole where he lay. Max shoveled in the hole and pressed the moss-covered earth down on top of it. He walked back five feet and examined his work. Other than for a few edges where he could see fresh dirt, it was as if nothing had happened there at all.

Back at the house he continued cleaning until he was satisfied it looked as if they had never been there. Next, he took a hot shower and changed his clothes, and a half hour later Max was driving down the driveway in the Jeep, a new wallet and passport with him, and almost four hundred dollars that he had found in the wallet, which, by the scale he was accustomed to, practically made him rich.

On the highway, Max stopped at a Burger King and ate until he felt sick. Then he drove straight to New York City, and a couple of blocks from Max W's apartment on Fourteenth Street, he found a parking garage and here he left the Jeep, wiping it down, the steering wheel and the dash and anything else he might have touched.

Max thought about going to Max W's apartment and seeing what he could find there, but it was too risky. For one, he'd forgotten to ask if Max W lived alone. He dropped the keys into a sewer.

That night he went to a dive bar in the Meatpacking District and there he met a pretty girl with brown eyes, and when she asked his name, he said out loud for the first time, "Max W."

"What's the *W* stand for?"

"Well, that I can't tell you. Not yet, anyway."

She took him home, which was the whole goal, and he told her after they fucked and he lay there feeling all verbal, the words just spilling out of him as they did sometimes after he came, that he was an artist and was going to be famous someday. She said she believed him. She said it sincerely. She said that she would believe anything he said.

When she left for her job as a bank teller in the morning, Max asked her if she minded if he slept in. She trusted him, because people always did.

He used her computer and googled Max Westmoreland, and Maxwell Westmoreland and even Max W, but nothing was out there saying he was missing, or anything else, and it would be a month or so before Max would find an article saying Max W was gone and friends and family were concerned.

But as far as Max knew, no one ever tied him to that great camp in the Adirondacks on that day in June. And it was as if Max W had just vanished.

That was how Max became him, or not him, for his plan was never to be fully Max W but his own Max W. There was one notable exception, and this was why he decided to adopt the name.

A few months later he wrote a letter to the California Institute of the Arts and gave Max's name and Social Security number and his own new address in New York and asked for copies of transcripts for both his BFA and MFA in painting.

When he created a résumé, it said he was a graduate with both degrees, and before long this child of the streets was hanging art in some of Manhattan's most prestigious galleries. He would shape and sculpt this narrative for years. He would borrow from his life and the one he took when it made sense to him. He was not Max W from Charleston, South Carolina, with the trust fund and the historic family camp in the mountains of New York. He was Max W from West Bumblefuck, New York, who lived homeless on the streets before becoming an artist.

One day Max was walking down a Chelsea street when he saw a bunch of kids sitting on the ledge of a building with their bags and their sign and their one scraggly dog. They were a group of crusty punks he used to run with. Max stopped in front of them and dropped a five into their bucket.

"Thanks, brother," this kid named Savage whom Max once hitch-hiked with for days on end said to him. For a moment Max thought he saw a glimmer of recognition in Savage's eyes but couldn't be sure. Max kept walking and Savage didn't say a thing. Max's transformation was complete.

Now, many years later, the plane circled above Burlington, Vermont. The rain had stopped, and below, Max could see the broad expanse of Lake Champlain, the small city below, and the craggy mountains on the other side of it. Somewhere beneath him were his house and his wife and his stepson. Max had no idea what he was coming home to. Down there was also someone who had figured out who he was, and now he needed to know not only who, but how much the person knew.

For Susannah, everything was normal about that day except for the note on the door. After she hung up with Max she placed the note in the cabinet where she kept her cigarettes—the cabinet of illicit things she tried to forget until she wanted them.

She went about the business of her day, working on her breathing, the way to take her back down. She was always trying to remember how to breathe again. She took a hot shower and then cobbled together for lunch what she called a refrigerator salad, a bit of this, a bit of that. She drank some wine. But the note was still there and it was almost as if she could hear it, those words speaking to her from behind the wood. It was kind of like a loud clock that just kept ticking in a silent house, the sound of it always the same, but the mind making it seem to grow louder and louder.

Susannah used to obsess about this sometimes. Not only how she could hear that ticking over and over but also this idea that the seconds themselves would never come back, as if they were things that appeared in the world and then vanished for eternity. *And what did you do with your life, Susannah?*

Now there was a note and she wondered what those words meant. Why did they scare her so much? After all, Max was probably right. It was nothing. Maybe it was someone's idea of a joke. Maybe the person even got the wrong house.

That afternoon, though, Susannah jumped when the doorbell rang. She went to the door and in her hand was her phone, ready for calling 911. But when she looked out through the glass, there was Freddy, her son, coming home from school. What could be more normal?

Susannah opened the door and he stood there looking exasperated. "Why's the door locked?"

"Oh," she said, as if surprised. "I must have done it by accident when I came back from my run."

Freddy didn't respond and went right to the kitchen, where he dumped his backpack and his skateboard on the counter and made himself a sandwich, a new thing for him, making sandwiches, ham and cheese on bread, drowning it with Russian dressing. He ate it with his earbuds in as if she weren't even there.

But today Susannah was grateful for this simple, predictable thing, and she knew as soon as he was done, he would disappear upstairs into his room and fall into his video-game world, which drove her crazy, but Max less so, Max saying the games are not as bad as they look. There were even some benefits, he said, but all Susannah saw was killing.

Though it was one of the things she loved about Max, how he related to Freddy. Max had proposed to Susannah six months after they met, in the exact same spot where she had first seen him come off the elevator. Lydia had summoned her to her apartment and Susannah was anticipating some small crisis, which was often the case when Lydia summoned her. Once she went all the way uptown because Lydia couldn't open a jar and was throwing a fit because she couldn't reach Tam, her housekeeper, who had the afternoon off.

But this time when the elevator opened into Lydia's apartment, Max was standing there with a big shit-eating grin on his face. Behind him was Lydia, as if she was orchestrating everything, which in some way she was.

"What is this?"

Max dropped to one knee.

"Oh, shit."

"Baby, I fell in love with you in this very spot, the moment I first saw you. I wasn't looking for love. I wasn't looking for anything, other than to meet Lydia. But there you were with those amazing eyes that I just fell into. I want you to be my wife. Will you marry me?"

Susannah put her hands over her face and cried. "You ready to be a dad? You always said you couldn't imagine it. Are you?"

"I love Freddy."

"Yes. Yes."

Behind Max, Lydia clasped her hands together and swept at her hair and Susannah went to Max and he slipped that antique ring that he found somehow on her finger. When he rose, they kissed and hugged while Lydia watched over them, the same way she watched over Max's career now.

Not that they had tons of money, but Susannah wanted a wedding. Max wanted to go down to City Hall and just knock it out. She had already done that once with Joseph and she didn't want that to be their story, too. Susannah had this idea of Freddy giving her away, the only family she had anymore, and this was Max's point as well, that he didn't have any family either, so why go through the motions of something?

She told him that he was thinking small for once. "We have all kinds of family, just not the conventional kind. Look at all these people we know."

So they compromised. They got married in the park with a handful of people watching, a pop-up wedding, and Max wore a dark suit and sneakers and the bride wore a used gown that miraculously fit her like a glove that she'd found at a thrift shop, and a veil that was once white but that had gone to gray over the years covering her face. They laughed about this—the almost-white wedding. Fitting to who they were.

Everyone they knew was ecstatic for them—"You guys are so perfect," people said, "so beautiful," which was how Susannah felt, blessed and lucky and perfect and beautiful. Everyone felt that way with the exception of her friend Rose. For some reason, she had never trusted Max, and it wasn't something they had talked about, but Susannah could read the distrust in her. Best friends are like that. Sometimes without even talking they can speak worlds to each other.

A couple of days before the ceremony, Susannah decided to call Rose on it. They were sitting outside at the Standard Grill, for a lunch neither of them could afford, but an indulgence they were trying to justify by the beauty of the day. "We'll order cheap," they said before they got seated, but then they were slurping oysters and drinking Prosecco and working through a large plate of thinly sliced Spanish ham and olives.

Rose always dressed loudly and that day was no exception: she had on a dress covered with giant red hearts and big red plastic loop earrings, her long black hair piled high in a bun over her round face.

Susannah brought it up almost casually. "You don't like Max."

"What? No." Rose dragged a piece of bread through the oil that had seeped out to the side of the plate of olives and ham. "I do like Max."

"I'm not sure I believe you."

"Susannah. Really."

"Come on, I know you. There's something you're not saying. I just want you to say it."

Rose sighed and looked out to the plaza in front of the hotel and below the High Line behind them. By looking north from their table they could see a slice of the plaza, full of people strolling on a beautiful day. Being in this section of Manhattan the two of them felt old. Everyone seemed so young and European and moneyed in their skinny jeans and the boys with the fade haircuts and their big white sneakers and the girls in skimpy sundresses and huge heels.

"It's just—" Rose stopped. "I don't know."

"He's kind to me."

"It's not that."

"Then what?"

Rose leaned forward. "How well do you know him, Susannah?"

"Max?"

"Yes, Max."

"I know it hasn't been that long. But I know his heart. You know what I mean? That doesn't always take so long. You can tell who someone is."

"But it's like he just appeared out of thin air, you know? Have you ever met any old friends of his? I mean, you haven't even met his mother."

"They're estranged. I, of all people, know what that's like."

"But think of all the people you know just here in New York. Does Max have any buddies he hangs out with? Some guys he went to college with? It just feels a little weird, that's all I'm saying."

"He was homeless as a teenager. He's wary of people, he told me that. And then he went to art school and it turned his life around. He was there on scholarship and not to make friends. It doesn't seem that weird to me."

"Okay. I am happy for you, you know that, right?"

"I do."

But then a month after the wedding, something curious happened that made Susannah recall that conversation with Rose.

It was Max's big night, his debut with Lydia, a joint show she had put together with G Spot, her protégé. G Spot's paintings were the headliner, big giant canvases with his primitive drawings and his graffiti and words etched across. They were already selling in the six figures before the show, and given the buzz around him, Lydia expected them to move.

Against this backdrop Lydia planned to introduce Max to the art world. She dedicated one entire wall to his word paintings, including the one he had made of Susannah the night they met.

Max was a natural at these things. Much more than G Spot, who looked the part but had the street artist's disdain of people and barely left a corner of the gallery all night. Max could work a room, as he had that first night at Lydia's. People were drawn to him the way they were to a good view. But not even Lydia knew that this was just the beginning, that the artist's statement he used that evening, written in clear language that began with "You are the art," would be the same simple words that would later launch him into the stratosphere.

Lydia priced his paintings low, very low for her gallery. They started at ten thousand dollars and the larger ones were closer to twenty thousand. Of the seventeen she chose to hang that night, eight of them sold, which was a huge opening for an unknown artist. Lydia was hustling as only she could—"This is going to be worth a quarter of a million in a year, Charles," Susannah overheard her saying to one well-known collector. "Get in now and think about it as an investment."

Susannah's life had never been more perfect than it was that night. She was in a beautiful wide white room in the middle of Manhattan, a room full of beautiful people high on champagne, and in the middle of it all was her beautiful, smart, charismatic husband. In less than an hour, they had made a good year's salary for the two of them.

Fucking pinch yourself, Susannah, she thought.

Afterward, a whole group went out to celebrate. With Susannah and Max was Rose and her man of the moment, Sid, an emergency-room doctor she had met on Tinder who was tall and thin and shy, and Nils, the squat Norwegian guy who had hung the show. They walked to the Breslin in the Ace Hotel. Rose ordered everyone mojitos and the bar was crowded and so was the restaurant and Susannah remembered how loud and happy they were.

They had one round of drinks and had ordered another and were standing crowded in a circle in the middle of the bar. Suddenly this guy with stringy long hair moved into their circle, bobbing like a drunk, moving from foot to foot, as if by standing still he would just fall over. He pushed Rose aside to get in front of Max, and he was shorter than Max, and stocky, and he looked up at Max, and he slurred when he spoke but he said, "Holy shit, Phil. I almost didn't recognize you. You got no hair. What the fuck happened to you?"

Max smiled at him. "My name is Max. Sorry."

The guy's face went blank for a minute, as if someone had just told him he was adopted. "Phil. What the fuck? It's me, Todd. I know you."

"I must have a doppelgänger." Max laughed. "Sorry, buddy."

Max turned his back on the guy and he walked away shaking his head and they all laughed about it. "I wish my name was Phil," Max said.

"Can you imagine?" Susannah said. "You as a Phil?" Everyone laughed at this, too.

But then they left the bar and were out on the street and starting to walk toward Madison and the guy was there again, this time grabbing Max on the shoulder to try to spin him around toward him.

"Phil," Susannah heard him say. "It's me, man."

They all tried to keep walking, the way you do when a homeless man confronts you.

Max did, too, for a moment. But then he turned quickly and Susannah didn't see it, but she somehow knew that Max had punched the guy in the face. The guy fell backward onto the side-walk and Susannah heard someone else who just happened to be walking by say, "Oh, shit."

Max was by her side again, shaking his right hand now and grimacing.

Next to Susannah, Rose looked stricken and said, "Jesus, why did you hit him?"

"He had a knife," Max said. "Let's keep walking, please."

Right then to their left was a young black guy, walking along-side Max and waving his finger in his face. "Yo, man, you can't just punch a dude and keep going. I saw that shit, man."

"Back off me," Max growled, and all of them kept walking briskly.

When they rounded the corner, Susannah felt her heart starting to race, the motor starting up, and she hoped she could stop it. So much energy was in the city. The streets were packed with people on a warm night. All around them—the lights and the stream of cars and the buildings—things felt suddenly as if they were closing in on her. Her new husband had just punched a man in the face in front of all of their friends. The man had a knife, Max had said. The man had a knife.

She didn't know if that was true, because no one else saw it. What she did know was that her husband was the kind of man who punched other men in the face and knocked them to the pavement. That was both terrifying but also strangely comforting. She wondered if it was okay to think that.

MAX RETURNED FROM CHICAGO A little after eight. It was no longer raining and Freddy was upstairs doing who knew what in his room, and while Susannah hoped it was homework, he was far more likely back on his video games or on his phone Snapchatting with his friends. But tonight she didn't care, and when Max keyed the door—for she still had it locked—she went to him and he smiled at her that smile that made her forget everything and he looked tired and she leaned up and kissed him and he took her in his arms.

"Where's Freddy?"

"Upstairs."

"I need a drink."

"Are you hungry?"

"Starving."

"Let me fix you something." Susannah was aware of the dance they were doing. In her mind she saw the note again, and it was as if those words hung in the air between them, big fat letters that were daring both of them to reach up and pull them down until they stood in front of them and they had to talk about them.

But for the moment it was nice not to. It was nice to have Max back, his quiet strength filling the room. He followed her into the kitchen and sat at the stool at the counter while first she made him a simple Manhattan, the way he liked it, mostly bourbon, and a splash of sweet vermouth, on the rocks.

While he sipped it, they made small talk, and she took a strip steak out of the fridge and salted it and heated a cast-iron pan on the stove. For years now Max had been pretty much carb-free in his eating, and this was what he liked: seared meat and some vegetables. Sometimes fish. Susannah liked to cook for him. She trimmed some asparagus and tossed them with olive oil. He talked about his trip. She half listened. A good crowd and his speech well received. Easier than talking about the weather, he said. The asparagus went into the hot oven, and with the cast-iron pan now hot Susannah laid the steak in there and it smoked good and fast but the fan sucked it out.

Something about her taking care of him this way was sexual. She found it empowering. *Lie back for me, honey, let me do the work.*

Susannah plated the steak and the asparagus and placed them in front of Max.

Max looked to the stairs and to where Freddy had not yet emerged. Then he looked down to his plate and sliced himself a piece of the meat.

"Show it to me."

"What?"

"The note."

Susannah went to the cabinet above the fridge and opened it. She reached up and grabbed that piece of paper and brought it over and placed it to the left of Max's plate. It was still folded. With his long fingers, Max opened it and studied it for what felt like a long time, as if somehow by just staring at that simple declarative sentence he would know what it meant.

He sighed. "I bet it's nothing."

"What could it be? I didn't want to drive myself crazy by trying to figure it out. But it's creepy, right?"

"Maybe. I don't know."

"It just felt like everything was going so well here."

"Everything is. This is some academic bullshit, that's all. I had some time to think on the plane. There's so much jealousy at the university—at every university. People who don't like how I am getting paid. Some who don't like what I do. Most of them are tired and old and no longer current. Fucking dinosaurs everywhere."

"So you think it was someone you work with?"

"Most likely."

Susannah walked behind Max and massaged his neck. "Why would they write that? 'I know who you are'?"

"I thought about that, too. Think about it. The title of my talk is 'You Are the Art.' They're trying to say I'm not an artist or something. It's an attempt to intimidate. Cowardly."

Suddenly, Susannah felt silly for being so afraid. Of course it was something like that. She kneaded his neck. Freddy swept into the kitchen, and seeing Max, Freddy smiled and Susannah found herself happy for the ease of the two of them, father, not father, friend. They fist-bumped.

"What's up, kid?" Max said, as if there were no worries at all.

Freddy shook his head, the teenager playing cool. "Nothing."

Max sipped his drink. Susannah felt the air of the day go out of her and all was well for now. Where there were once two, there were now three. It was only a note on the door. No one had a thing on them. This was how they loved, she told herself. A small tribe, they were. No one was getting in.

THE THING ABOUT THE TWO of them, Max felt, was that marriage had never dulled their edges. Even when Susannah was having a bad day and she became flighty like a songbird, he could always ground her in sex. He never lost his desire for her. Years in, he wanted her just as much as on that first night when she dropped her clothes in his apartment and stood there golden and nude in front of him. They had chemistry, and when people asked Max about it, he would joke that despite what they say in school, you can't really teach chemistry.

That night when he returned from Chicago, Max was the one who needed her. Susannah was a mess: he could see it in her eyes, how they darted back and forth. She was acting like a caged squirrel. He had always tried to shield her from things, and if he had found the note, he probably wouldn't have showed it to her. Max didn't view this as dishonest. *We can all handle what we can handle*, he thought.

After Freddy went to bed, Max brought Susannah upstairs, led her by the hand. When they reached the bedroom door, he presented the game. He turned and whispered to her, "Who are we tonight?"

She looked up at him and smiled. "You're the handyman in my building who has come to see why my shower doesn't work."

"And who are you?"

"I'm the terribly bored cliché of a housewife who is alone because her famous husband is always traveling to places like Chicago to give speeches."

Max laughed and took her into the room and closed the door behind them. "Ma'am," he said, in a vaguely working-class New York accent, "I can fix your shower, but I need to get some parts first. Is there anything I can do to help you while we wait?"

"Since my husband is away, would you mind helping me with this zipper? I'm afraid I can't reach it myself."

They moved into each other, and for a moment, away from the rest of things. *It's amazing,* thought Max, *how powerfully the imagination, especially when you are pretending to be something you are not, becomes an escape from the trivia of life.*

SOMETIME IN THE BLUE OF that night Max woke with a start. Out the windows it was still dark. He leaned up on his elbows and looked at Susannah. She was facing away from him, curled up, her mouth open with the softest of snores, a little catch in her throat. Strands of red hair fell down the side of her face and across her cheek.

Max stared at her for a while, then he slowly rose out of bed and pulled a T-shirt over his head, and wearing that and the pajama pants he slept in, he stepped outside the room and into the hallway. He walked past Freddy's door and padded silently down the stairs. The house was quiet and still.

In the kitchen he stepped into a pair of mud boots, then he opened the back door and stepped outside and onto the stone patio. The air was mild and the grass smelled sweet from the previous day's rain. It was dark but gray, and looking up, Max couldn't see any stars. He walked out into the yard and turned and looked back at his house. Upstairs was the window to their bedroom, where Susannah slept oblivious to her being alone now. It was a stately house, and from this perspective, Max saw it with new eyes, as others might have seen it. Moments where it sank in that he actually lived here, that he had pulled this thing off. That in reality it wasn't all that long ago that he sat down on Church Street in the summers, about a half mile down the hill from where he now stood, traveling through since Burlington was one of the cities they all knew about, a sanctuary for kids such as him. It was a place where he could huddle against the side of a building with some fellow travelers, a few ratty dogs, and a cup in his hand extended out to the straight world.

Max walked around the house and through a break in the tall arborvitae that separated the driveway from the backyard. He walked into the driveway, past their one car, a Volkswagen wagon he'd bought when they left New York, and out to the street.

For a while he just stood there, in the middle of the quiet neighborhood in the dark. If anyone had happened upon him, Max might have looked like any old suburban dad who had forgotten to take out the trash, standing in the road in pajamas and mud boots. He felt the damp warmth of the spring night on his skin. He looked down his street toward where it met Main Street, and he could only faintly hear the distant traffic. He looked around his sleeping neighborhood, all these grand homes, up here high on the hill. All of them had made it, hadn't they? They had climbed the hill, and he meant to stay here. There was the tree-lined street, and the beautiful houses, and inside, like the steeples children make with their fingers, all the sleeping families. *Just as it should be,* thought Max.

MAX NORMALLY LOVED HIS CLASSROOM. From it he could look out and see the town below and then beyond to the wide flat blue of the massive lake. He usually loved teaching. He had come to love the sound of his own voice, throwing pointed questions at the students, challenging them with the Socratic method, working without a net as he liked to say, no real lesson plan, just a set of images he projected with his computer onto the large screen and then go from there, see where the ideas took them, the collective consciousness of teacher and students coming together into something larger than themselves. This is what Max told himself on the good days when he believed his own bullshit.

But in class the morning after returning from Chicago, he had zero focus. It was as if his voice came from somewhere else, and then the debate that followed his intro was just a shrill cacophony filling the air.

In a short time, Max's classes had become popular. There was a buzz about them. The students called him Max, at his request. He understood that some were there just because of how he looked—a majority of the art majors were young women, and he'd read the comments online, on websites where students rated teachers. He was not unaware of the power this gave him and he was determined to wield it cautiously, especially in relation to his colleagues.

Max muddled through class, and afterward, walking on a pathway through the central quadrangle, he looked around at the coeds moving in all different directions around him. They were bright-faced kids, the bunch of them, and not for the first time he was aware of the gift of this academic life, how perfectly it had all come together. Even if he wasn't still on the street, he would be lucky to work in some soulless office, or hawking Buicks somewhere, spending winter mornings brushing off rows of cars after a snowstorm.

Max felt a hand on his shoulder and turned to see Terry Germaine, a sound artist also in the art department who served on the committee that had hired Max.

"Ready to be bored silly?" Terry asked. "Some good consensus decision making?"

"Always. Nothing like a department meeting on a sunny day," Max continued, as if he had sat through hundreds of them when in reality this would be only his third one ever.

Max surreptitiously studied Terry in profile as they walked, his bald head and his absurdly long salt-and-pepper beard, a cultivated look, to be sure, just as Max's was, the carefully crafted uniforms that shout, *Hey, we are artists and we don't give a shit what anyone else thinks.* Terry, as if aware of Max's gaze, turned toward him and gave him an awkward half smile, and Max wondered if Terry was the one.

Max tried to imagine Terry sneaking up toward Max's house with a pre-taped note, placing it against the wood of the door before skulking off down the street.

No, Terry may be wary of my sudden notoriety and wish it for himself, but he doesn't have the balls to take me on, thought Max. *He is way too soft.*

They climbed the steps of the red stone building that housed the art department. Inside they passed students staring at bulletin boards, and together the two went upstairs to the department offices.

In a small room with two wooden tables pushed together, everyone else had already gathered, the other four full-time artists: Ernst Werner, the department chair, a German impressionist in his late sixties; Susan Lin, a petite Chinese American with her hair cut dramatically in a bowl who did video work; David Hammer, who did ephemeral installations made from cut-up paper; and finally, Jean Littleton, her hair still long and blond in her late sixties, who was probably closest to Max academically since she didn't make anything, but had become famous as a feminist thinker when she created a series of happenings in New York in the early seventies. Jean had grown bitter over the years. Of all of them she was the only one who remotely frightened him, for along with her generalized anger at the world, she could see through people. Max worried she thought he was a poser, though she also liked to make a show of not tolerating straight white men.

But Jean wouldn't leave a note on his door. That wasn't her style. She loved confrontation. Her entire career had been built on it. So Max could dismiss her, cross her off the list. But the others were all suspects.

He and Terry sat down. Max looked around the room as Ernst led them through "his process," which meant raising concerns and then stopping and listening thoughtfully while others talked. Ernst's commitment was that all decisions would be group ones built on consensus, and that if anyone opposed a particular idea, they would talk it through until all agreed. Max hadn't seen it in action yet, but he had heard war stories about meetings that went on ten or more hours, a bunch of artist academics deliberating like a hung jury over trivial matters such as specific word choices in a letter they intended to send to the dean about an appointment. Beautiful.

Ernst was prattling on about some new policy the provost was talking about implementing. Ernst was Paleolithic to Max, exactly the kind of artist the art world fawned over in a different time; a talent for what he did, for sure, but also banal and derivative of all the great moderns. His work still sold modestly in New York, but mostly the sun had set on his career. He had his sailboat he lived on in the summer, moving up and down the large lake with his husband, who was some twenty-five years younger and had once, naturally, been a student of his.

It wasn't Ernst either.

That left David Hammer or quiet Susan Lin. A case could be made for either. David used to be the only handsome youngish heterosexual guy, and this was not to be underestimated. While David was always friendly in his vaguely Southern way (David was originally from Georgia), Terry Germaine had told Max that David had opposed Max's hiring, saying at the time that the project that had first brought him to prominence, a set of interviews he did with the homeless on a simple recording device, a project that had been bought by MoMA, was not even art, but rather some kind of "faux documentary."

As for Susan, who once made a film that was three hours of her expressionless face, which she called *All You Need to Know About Chinese Oppression You Can See Right Here*, Max doubted that she had the same issues with his work. Then again, perhaps she felt he was encroaching on her space, especially with his refrain that the personal was always political. For what Max had learned was that while art education encouraged a fealty to a specific kind of thinking, within that there tended to be room for only one practitioner per individual tranche of thought. Someone had to be the most feminist, someone had to tackle the plight of indigenous peoples, and someone had to take on poverty and injustice.

The only thing Max stuck to as any kind of principle was to forbid his students to use the word *beauty*, even though secretly he loved the word. "It's too easy," he told his classes. "The B-word doesn't mean anything so I never want to hear it in my class." Susan Lin agreed with this, too, so maybe she didn't like his stealing her thunder.

Max was so lost in thought with all this he didn't realize that he had chuckled out loud.

"Max?" Ernst said. "You think we should be handling this differently?"

Max shook his head, since he didn't even know what was being discussed. "No," he said, gambling, "I think this is perfectly right."

"Okay, good," said Ernst. "Others?"

What had made Max laugh was an image of Susan Lin moving stealthily down the dewy lawns on his street, dressed in her customary black turtleneck and black jeans to put a note on his door, this tiny woman hiding in front of bushes. Max didn't even know where she lived and had never thought of it before. Though if he had to guess, it was most likely in one of those industrial-loft developments a town away where the Winooski River ran over a set of dams. She would have to drive. David Hammer, on the other hand, lived one block away, in a house similar to Max's. He had a dog, some pit-bull-looking mutt he walked around with. Once, last fall, Max had invited him up for a drink when Max and Susannah were sitting on the porch and David and his pooch came down the street.

David was talking now, that slight drawl tempered by a decade in New York and Vermont, and Max didn't hear a word he said, more inane blather about something Max could not care less about. But as David talked, Max did study him and thought, *Yes, it must be David.* David, who played like a child with paper and scissors and geometric shapes, as if he had graduated from making snowflakes to something just beyond that and never went any further.

After the meeting came to a merciful and early end, Max stepped out of the building and called to David, who was in front of him walking briskly toward the library. David stopped and Max broke into a half jog to catch up to him.

"Hey," Max said. "Wondering if you have plans this weekend? It would be good to have you over. You and your wife, I'm sorry, I don't remember her name."

"Joanie."

"Yes, of course. Joanie. What do you think? We haven't gotten enough of a chance to talk."

"Well, that's nice of you. I don't think we have anything Saturday, but I need to check with Joanie. Get back to you?"

"Sure."

Max watched David retreat from him, that urgent fast walk of his, standing straight up. Above, the sky was completely cloudless and the palest of blues and the sun was spring warm on Max's face.

Keep your enemies closer, thought Max, *until you find out how to get rid of them.*

THAT SATURDAY NIGHT THEY HAD a dinner party with David Hammer and his wife, Joanie. Susannah had not met them before, and she was charmed by their Georgian accents, that slow-Southern talking way, but after they had been there for a short time, she found herself having a hard time with Joanie. She was strung tighter than a violin. She looked like a bird, black haired and slight, pointy nosed and always looking as if she were going to jump out of her skin. She was a lawyer at one of the downtown firms.

When Max first told her they were coming, Susannah brightened. It made everything seem normal again, and she imagined cooking a paella all day, with sausages and mussels, the one she had watched her mother make on special occasions when Susannah was a girl. Then Max told her he was pretty sure they were both vegans.

"Oh, Jesus."

"How can you tell who at the party is a vegan?" Max asked, his eyes twinkling.

"How?"

"Don't worry, they'll find you. 'Is this vegan?' . . . 'Is this vegan?'"

"Very funny. But what am I going to cook?"

He kissed Susannah's forehead. "You'll figure it out."

Susannah googled best vegan recipes and ended up cooking some pasta with wild mushrooms and made a salad. The evening was beautiful and warm and they ate out on the wraparound porch. Freddy had his friend Miles over, and the two of them were upstairs and didn't join. David and Joanie didn't have children.

"I got a vasectomy when I turned eighteen," David said.

"No shit," said Max. "You really knew yourself."

David shrugged. "Yeah, not sure I wanted to keep populating a dying planet." He looked at Susannah. "No offense. I mean, doesn't bother me that others have children."

Just as it probably doesn't bother you that other people eat meat, Susannah thought. "No offense taken," Susannah said. "And you, Joanie, any regrets?"

"Not really. I never had that bug."

David said, "So, Max, what years were you at CalArts again? The early aughts?"

"Yeah. Graduated in '04."

"So you must have worked with Karl Banks then?"

"I didn't."

"But I thought you studied painting? He's pretty much the man out there."

"I knew who he was, of course. But I kind of kept to myself."

David nodded, as if taking this in. "You guys must miss New York."

"Not at all," Susannah said. "There are some things I miss. Like good bagels. But it's so lovely here. And it's especially been good for Freddy."

"I miss the anonymity sometimes," Max said. "Walking down streets where no one knows who you are."

"Really?" David said. "That surprises me. You seem quite comfortable in the limelight, Max."

Max didn't respond to this, and Susannah thought the comment was deliberately snarky. Max asked, "How about you guys? Do you miss Atlanta? You were at Emory, right?"

"Yes, Emory. I think we miss the weather. We're still not crazy about the winters."

"The summers are lovely, though," Joanie said. "Especially the lake. I've always loved lakes. More than the ocean."

Max poured more wine and they jabbered on, Joanie complimenting Susannah's food, all small talk, and it should have been pleasant, dining outside for the first time since the fall, but suddenly Susannah became aware of everyone breathing. They were breathing like crickets, she thought, the rise and fall of it all, in between words and bites of food. What was it that made them human?

Susannah looked across at David, his pleasant face, the blocky glasses, and then she looked at Max. Max was intently focused on him. It was one of his talents, his ability to engage with others, let them believe, for a moment, that their words were the most important words being uttered anywhere. But tonight Susannah saw a different quality to Max's gaze.

Max's eyes were electric. Blue darts of hate.

Susannah suddenly realized that this was why they were here tonight, on her porch, eating vegan pasta and drinking red wine. It seemed so obvious she wondered why she hadn't picked up on it before. Max thought David had left the note.

A feeling of dread overcame her, this idea that Max was going to do something awful. But Susannah told herself that she was reading too much into everything again, something Joseph used to tell her in therapy. She hated it when he said that, for she always felt that he was gaslighting her when he did this.

When she told him so, Joseph would say, "This is exactly what I mean, Susannah."

The circular logic continued and she wasn't equipped to fight it. He was too calm, too reasonable, and too expert.

Now, listening to the conversation going around, which had, inevitably, turned to work and the politics of the art department, Susannah heard Joseph's words in her head. Telling her to breathe, that it would all be okay, that the world kept spinning whether we want it to or not.

AFTER THE HAMMERS LEFT, WHICH was sometime around eleven, Susannah and Max were in the kitchen. He was doing the dishes and she had snuck out for a cigarette before coming back in. Freddy had popped in for a minute to grab some of the cookies Susannah had put out earlier, then disappeared back upstairs. This was the thing about teenagers, she thought sometimes. How quickly they become stealthy people in your own house, the little boy who was once her shadow now making himself invisible.

Max was rinsing the plates and loading the dishwasher. Susannah sat on top of the counter and watched him work. She liked this about him, that he was good about this stuff, the little domestic things, pitching in.

"So that was fun," Susannah said a little sarcastically.

He turned his head, looked at her where she sat. "It was."

"I had a realization partway through dinner."

"What's that?"

"That you think David is the one who left the note."

"He's not."

"You don't think?"

"No," Max said. "I did before. And you're right. That's why I invited them over."

"But there was a little bite to what he was saying to you, don't you think? The stuff about how you need attention?"

"That's how I know it's not him."

"I don't follow."

"Well, if it was him, he would do everything he could not to reveal himself. No biting comments. No thinly veiled jealousy. Unless he couldn't control himself, which I doubt. Those two are very controlled."

"I kept trying to imagine them fucking."

Max laughed. "What?"

"I do that sometimes with couples. Picture them in bed. Or try to."

"What did you decide?"

"She's definitely a dead fish. Just lies there."

"I'm not sure he's that much more alive," Max said.

"I bet he never takes those glasses off. Probably sleeps in them. Total back sleeper. Can't tell if he's awake or not."

"Amazing." Max laughed. Then he came over to her, drying his hands on a towel. He put the towel on the counter, leaned forward, and pecked her on the lips. "Speaking of bed . . ."

"Take me with you."

THEY DIDN'T HAVE SEX THAT night, and maybe if they had, Susannah could have beaten back the thoughts that started to swirl.

They dressed for bed and side by side brushed their teeth, then Susannah went to check on Freddy. By the time she got back, Max was snoring on his side, his face pressed into the pillow.

She lay next to him and tried to read the book from her night table, one of those book-club reads that everyone was discussing, the messed-up girl who sees things and everyone thinks she is crazy and it turns out she's not. But mostly Susannah just found the girl annoying and her mind started to drift. She turned off the bedroom light and the room was dark and she curled into Max and he stirred slightly.

Within moments she knew she had made a mistake by turning off the light, for this was the thing about panic, she could tell when it was coming. It was like seeing a storm off in the distance and you know you should run and you don't. Tonight, her inability to focus on the book told her all she needed to know.

She started replaying the dinner from just hours before and that feeling she had had of being trapped, as if she were stuck on her own porch somehow. That moment when she became aware of them all breathing.

Many years ago, Joseph tried to make a point to her. He was frustrated, he said, by her failure to progress, as if she were in labor, she thought, and about to birth some kind of new her if only she pushed hard enough.

They were in his office. It was winter, maybe January. Outside, the day was gray and sad. Susannah's mood had been the same and they had had a fight, or that might be the wrong term because Joseph never fought. He deflected. But Susannah was angry with him and she had sat in her chair yelling at him about something that must have been ultimately inconsequential since later she wouldn't remember that part of the conversation.

But Joseph started to lecture her, pedantically, in her view, about this and that, and she ignored him, refusing to make eye contact, and turning her eyes toward the window, to the city outside those closed-in walls.

Susannah vaguely remembered seeing him rise out of his chair and move to his desk to her left, against the far wall. She heard him open the top drawer.

When she looked up, he was moving toward her with a gun in his hand. Susannah didn't even know he had a gun.

"What the fuck, Joseph?"

"Sit down. Relax. This is therapy."

"Why do you have a gun?"

He ignored this and pressed the barrel of the pistol into the side of her head. She looked up at him and began to cry.

"I can read your mind."

"What are you saying?" she said between tears. "What is this?"

"Susannah, listen to me. This is important. I can read your mind."

"I haven't done anything."

"I want you to think of a white bear."

"A white bear?"

"Yes, a white bear. Can you picture it?"

She was breathing hard and his voice was suddenly melodic and she did what he said. "Yes. I can picture it."

"I can tell."

"What is this? What are you doing?"

"Think of the white bear, Susannah." His voice was different, stony and serious. "Just like that."

And she was, thinking of the white bear, seeing it standing up, tall and pale and magnificent, while the metal point of the gun was pressed against her head, right above her ear.

"I'm going to count down from ten. And when I reach one, if you are still thinking of the white bear, you are dead."

"Jesus, Joseph."

"Ten, nine, eight . . ."

Susannah's mind raced. She looked frantically around the room. The light from the lamp on the stand next to his chair was yellow. *Yellow lamp,* she said to herself. *White bear.* It wouldn't go away.

". . . seven, six, five, four . . ."

She made herself say *yellow lamp* over and over in her head, but the bear wouldn't leave, vaguely formed, but there, all of it.

". . . three, two, one."

The trigger clicked emptily. Joseph lowered his hand to his side. Susannah screamed and flailed her arms and legs like a toddler on an unwelcome time-out.

Joseph walked slowly to his chair and sat in it. He looked at her. He sighed. His voice was resigned. "You couldn't do it."

She wanted to come at him but she was too fucked up to move. "You asshole."

"I was making a point, an important one."

"You pointed a fucking gun at my head."

"Yes, I did. But the white bear, Susannah. It is always there. It will always be there. You must learn to live with it. It will never kill you. In fact, if you want, you even get to hunt it. We can talk about what that means. You get to choose."

She felt the breath come back into her body. The fear had done something to her. Joseph had changed her. He had altered her mind, the very chemical composition of it, once again.

Susannah wanted to fucking hate him. But she saw the way he looked at her and she looked at his handsome, wrinkled face and those soulful eyes were full of empathy. Now that it was over, his voice, especially, was calming her again, talking her to sleep.

THE
SECOND
NOTE

MAX DID NOT CONSIDER HIMSELF an evil person. If anyone had asked him about it, he might have rejected the entire idea of evilness, seeing it as too simple a construct. If pinned down, he would say he just saw the world differently. That he had a greater understanding of things that came through living outside it all.

Max rejected history as a narrative of constant progress. He believed people confused technological innovation and comfort with actual progress. For when you stripped it all away, Max believed, we were what we had always been: tribal peoples just trying to survive and make sure our own do the same. We were all hunters on the plains of life, bringing back food for the village.

To his mind that meant doing things outside the bounds of conventional morality, some of them large, and some of them small, to achieve this objective. He was not in the habit of lying to Susannah.

But lie to Susannah he did, and he did it, he believed, to protect her. Parts of her were harder than diamonds, and other parts shattered like glass. Max supposed that was true of everyone, and being married sometimes means knowing which of those things you keep from the other for the greater good.

For Max, not telling her the truth after the Hammers left was easier than sleep. He knew it was David Hammer who had left the note. Max saw it in David's eyes. And Max heard it in the questions—asking him about CalArts and trying to walk him into a trap. He smelled it in David's general disdain, which after a few drinks he hid worse than a two-bit magician.

What Max didn't know was how much David Hammer actually knew—and whom he might have told. Did his uptight wife know? Had he told other people at the university?

Max's hunch was that David didn't know much. Maybe he'd discovered that Max had lied about his degrees. But if David had told anyone at the university, Max would certainly know by now. Those things were not taken lightly. He would have been summoned to the dean's office and sent packing the same day, with a security guard to observe as he filled boxes and removed them from campus. The locks changed. No, David Hammer hadn't done that. Yet.

Instead he had chosen to screw with Max, and for reasons he didn't know. Perhaps David thought he was clever, and this was fun for him. Was a sadist hiding behind that polite Southern drawl?

Max spent that Sunday tossing those thoughts around in his mind, while around him Susannah and Freddy were oblivious of his internal musings. It was a beautiful spring day, with a warm breeze coming off the lake and a light chop when you looked out across to the mountains. Susannah forced Freddy—who wanted nothing to do with it—to ride the ferry out of Charlotte with his parents over to the New York side of the lake and the little village of Essex. People had been telling them they should do this since they had moved here. It was the perfect, easy day trip.

They had lunch at a restaurant on the Essex dock and watched the sailboats going by, tacking back and forth against the wind. Afterward they poked around some small stores and art galleries. The art was what Max expected—touristy as shit, competent landscapes for rich people who wanted to put the same view they saw every day inside their houses.

At a little used-furniture place, Susannah insisted on buying a small stool that was half-covered with splotchy paint. Max mildly objected, not knowing why she even wanted it, but it was beautiful out and she looked lovely and happy, and even surly Freddy was staying off his phone. Max also knew that a day such as this wasn't complete unless you could later point to some artifact and say it reminded you of the way the sun felt that afternoon. Max lugged it around the rest of the day and was grateful when they got back to the other side and the car and he could let it go.

There was something about a bright, lovely spring day. They were all in great spirits. That night Max even cooked for them—well, grilled, since he was no pro in the kitchen. But he made cheeseburgers, and while they were cooking, Susannah came and leaned into him and looked up at him with those candy eyes and that big smile and it was as if none of this were happening.

The next morning, Max had a nine-fifteen class. He liked to go by his office beforehand and open his door and leave it open. This small, calculated move let the chair, who always came in around nine thirty, know that Max had already been there. If he had tenure, he wouldn't have given a shit. But even with the stature of his appointment, he knew it was not to be taken for granted. He and Susannah liked it here too much.

She was in the kitchen drinking her cappuccino when he left the house. Freddy had been gone for a while since he picked up the bus at seven forty-five out on Main Street. Max came rushing out the front door with his messenger bag over his shoulder and most days he probably wouldn't have seen it. But for some reason today he turned and looked at the door after he closed it behind him, and there, three-quarters of the way up it, was a piece of paper folded in half and taped to the wood.

Max stepped back and quickly snatched it and clasped it in his hand and kept walking. On the off chance Susannah was looking out the window, he wanted to get far enough away from the house so she couldn't see before he read it.

Halfway down the block, he stopped. He looked around. The street was empty. Max took the piece of paper from his hand and opened it.

It had the same big blocky letters.

DID YOU GET AWAY WITH IT?

David Hammer, you coward. Game on, Max said under his breath. He put the note in his pocket and walked toward Main Street. He climbed the hill to the university and went on into the meat of it, students streaming all around him on the paved walkways.

MAX WAS NOT IMMUNE to guilt or regret. In the early years after the Adirondacks, he sometimes dreamed of the original Max W, seeing him not as he looked in that moment before the glass met his face, but with his wide smile when he pulled over that fateful day and picked Max up on the side of I-95.

But later, it was as if it never happened, and if not for the occasional article you could find if you searched on *Maxwell Westmoreland*—*Max W* searches only turned up him—it was almost as if he never existed. This child of wealth and privilege who was trying to be a painter and was just ripped out of the world. And there hadn't been anything in years. The last piece Max had found was from the Charleston's *Post and Courier,* under the headline "Area Family Has Not Given Up Hope in Finding Missing Son."

It talked about how Max W was last seen by the local sheriff at his family summer home in upstate New York. But that he had returned to New York City and was thought to have disappeared there. That he was an eccentric and wealthy young man who had always been running from his family. One theory among his friends was that he had moved to Alaska and was living under an assumed name. Apparently, he had an obsession with Alaska, of getting as far away from his family and the money as possible. That he loved the land and hunting and wanted no part of society.

Sometimes Max liked to think of Max W there. Living on the edge of some primordial forest, catching salmon from brackish rivers, and hunting deer and moose. Max pictured him painting away the shortened days and finding a boyfriend to make the long winters more tolerable.

This was the beauty of being an artist, Max thought. You could imagine things into being. You don't only reflect reality through art, you also get to create it, which is what he told his students over and over. Max's life was living proof of that.

Max ran into David Hammer after lunch. He was coming out of Chittenden Hall, one of the classroom buildings. Max was out front, talking to two female students from one of his classes. He saw David Hammer out of the corner of his eye, black jacket and white shirt on. His jacket matched the frames of his glasses.

"Excuse me," Max said to the two young women, and hailed, "David, hey."

David Hammer stopped, waited for Max, and smiled weakly. Max looked for any signs in his body language. But he was good. A pro at holding himself together, though Max was going to show him what a real actor was like. Anyone can pretend to be angry, or sad, but the bigger trick was never showing that you were.

"That was fun the other night, man," David Hammer said.

"It was. Thanks for coming."

"Appreciate you having us. You have class now?"

"No, just office hours this afternoon."

David Hammer nodded. "I've got a two-hour studio. Grind."

"It beats working."

"True."

"Hey, listen," said Max. "The other night you were talking about trail running. I wonder if I could come with you sometime. Seems like a great way to keep in shape and get outdoors."

David Hammer looked Max up and down skeptically. "I didn't know you ran. I've been doing it a long time. I go pretty hard."

"I'll keep up."

"How about Saturday then? You free?"

"I am."

"I'll pick you up at nine."

"Perfect," Max said.

"See you then."

Watching David as he walked away, Max felt as if perhaps he had won something. David was writing the notes but hadn't gone to anyone else, yet. Max could tell David hadn't. He was way too pleased with himself. More important, Max had time.

And now David Hammer was going to show how fast he could run to Max.

Susannah believed in small secrets. Tiny things you do. One of hers was that she liked to watch Max out the window when he walked to work. She also liked, if she knew when he was expected home, to look out the window to see him coming down the street, that moment when she anticipated his arrival, saying to herself, *Any minute now he will come into view,* and then there he was, that confident stride that she loved. *Isn't it funny,* she thought, *that you recognize your man just by the way he walks?*

Max had no idea this was something she did. Susannah did it for a simple reason: she wanted to appreciate him. How often do people get to just watch the one they love when the person is unaware of their gaze?

A window in the foyer looked down the street. In the mornings Susannah would stand here and watch until he was out of sight on his way to the university. On his return, she stood here until he got close, then she faded into the kitchen as if she weren't expecting him, as if she had better things to do with her afternoon than just hope he would be home.

That Monday morning, as usual, she watched Max leave. She watched him bound off the porch with his long strides and onto the sidewalk. But that day something was different. At first, Susannah saw it in his face, a brief glimpse of his profile before he moved beyond her view. His face looked tight, clenched, as if he were chewing on something hard. She had seen this before, a tenseness that could come over him in moments and that he tried to hide from others. Usually it emerged in moments of anger, such as when she pushed him on something, and early in their relationship when it crept across his face, sometimes Susannah worried he might strike her. But he never did. That wasn't Max.

It was more that, she learned over time, he had to steel himself against anger. Max was complicated. All the great men were, Susannah thought, not that she had known many that she would put in that category besides Max. She had heard that somewhere. But underneath that electric charm lay a thick ribbon of anger. They were the flip sides of the same coin, right? Could you have one without the other? Susannah had never seen it.

So, in that way, Max was not an exception. But as time passed with them, as he became more and more in demand, as his dreams started to come true, ambitions realized through both hard work and an innate ability to speak to people, Susannah saw this side of him less and less, as if it was not getting those things that made him tight, which she interpreted as more proof of his greatness, for many people, she thought, would find greater strain in success.

But that morning it was all over his face. As she stood by the foyer window, her heart clenched when she realized why, or at least thought she realized why, she couldn't be sure.

For in his hand she saw the card he held, the carefully folded piece of paper, and while at the distance she was viewing this, maybe fifteen yards, she shouldn't have known what it was. But she did, because one morning not long ago she had held a similar piece of paper in her hands.

There was a second note.

What did it say? And why wasn't Max coming back to tell her about it?

Susannah practiced her breathing. Those deep yoga breaths, long on the exhale. She brought her cappuccino to her lips and sipped from the frothy milk. She wanted to call Max and ask him, but she also knew he was on his way to class. *He will text me,* she told herself. *Relax. He doesn't know you saw him.*

But all morning she waited to hear from him—and nothing. She forced herself to run, but even running, she couldn't stop thinking about it, moving down along the gray lake, surrounded by such beauty, but all she saw was those blocky letters, that careful script: the words of someone tormenting them. What did it say this time?

After lunch, Susannah couldn't wait any longer and texted him. She kept it simple; it was his job to come to her. *How is your day?*

Good, he wrote right back. *Busy.*

Anything going on?

Just the usual.

Susannah was out back, having one of those precious cigarettes she rationed out to herself. She was staring at the manicured backyard, the flower gardens that lined it, the fresh wood chips that Max had had the landscapers put down last week, shiny and brown against the perfect green edges. Why wasn't he telling her? Maybe Max was just waiting to do so in person. But unlike watching him out the window out of love, this was not a secret he could keep. It affected all of them—Max and Freddy and her, their family.

AFTER SCHOOL, FREDDY HAD A dentist appointment. He didn't want to go, even though they had discussed it in the morning. Driving in the car down traffic-filled Shelburne Road, Susannah tried to draw him out about school. He didn't talk about it much. But she was not worried. Freddy might have had a hot mess of a haircut and an addiction to video games, and he never seemed to study hard, but he always did well. School was easy for him, which it certainly never was for her. With what appeared minimal effort, he got all A's and B's. Clearly, his ability to ratchet up the focus when he needed it he got from Joseph.

At a red light, Susannah turned and looked at him. He had his headphones on, as he almost always did, and she could faintly hear the beat of the hip-hop that was blasting in his head. His hair fell down over his eyes, and for a brief moment he pushed it unconsciously out of the way and she saw how pretty he was. This boy she had made, with long lashes and dark Spanish eyes.

While Freddy got his teeth cleaned, Susannah tried to stay busy in the dentist's waiting room. She kept checking her phone, thinking, *Come on, Max, tell me. Tell me everything.* But her phone was silent. She tried to busy herself with trashy magazines but had a hard time focusing even on the bullshit things that are written for people who can't focus—"56 Ways to Please Your Man!" "Is Your Guy a Narcissist? Take This Quiz!"

Freddy came out and they drove home. He disappeared upstairs with his headphones on. This was the thing, Susannah thought, about being a stay-at-home mom with a teenager: there were vast caverns of time. She looked at the clock. It was four fifteen. Max would be home around five thirty. An hour and fifteen minutes, given the circumstances, felt eternal. Maybe this was why people took pills or drank to kill the time.

Susannah rifled through the fridge, pulling out things she could cobble together for dinner: a package of chicken legs, some baby carrots, a head of kale. She preheated the oven and broke the chicken down into pieces of legs and thighs and seasoned these with salt and pepper and smoked paprika, the way her mother used to do. Susannah rubbed them down with olive oil. She roasted them on high heat so that the skin would be crisp and the meat, moist. She put water on to boil for the carrots. The kale she chopped small, to sauté with onions and garlic. Freddy would eat the chicken and pretend to pick at the rest.

The cooking helped. For the first time that day, Susannah felt her vision broaden, and the nagging pounding in her chest, the bear wanting to rise, seemed to slow to the tiniest of drumbeats. It reminded her of the importance of simple things. What it feels like to take care of people. When Joseph died, Susannah missed him tremendously, but the thing she missed more was being a wife. She knew that didn't sound particularly feminist, but for her it was true. She liked being part of something bigger than herself, and she didn't care if anyone else disapproved.

MAX WAS A LITTLE LATE that night, but Susannah still managed to see him coming down the street, her day now bookended by these moments of staring out the window. Outside, it was a beautiful spring evening, the days longer now and the sun still high in the sky. He had a bounce in his step almost, moving quickly, and Susannah saw him shout out to the Larsens, neighbors of theirs who were on their porch. He gave them his best broad smile. Gone was all the tightness she had seen in his face earlier.

She went back to the kitchen. A moment later the door opened, and for some reason she caught her breath as she heard his footfalls coming through the foyer and into the kitchen.

He came toward her. "Something smells good."

"Roast chicken."

"Yum. I'm famished."

He was all large and charming and full of life: the magnificent Max, a man without a care in the world. This was not the same person, Susannah observed, who had pulled a second note off their door earlier today and then grimaced as if he had come home to find his beloved dog dead in the kitchen.

His buoyancy continued through dinner. Susannah almost got swept up in it. Freddy definitely did, the two of them joking and laughing. She studied Max for clues. His eyes were so bright, almost manic. Then he told her he had seen David Hammer earlier and he had complimented her on her cooking.

"That was nice of him."

"Yeah, we're actually going to go running on Saturday."

"Running?"

Max was not a runner. Sometimes he did push-ups in the morning before he got in the shower, but that was generally the extent of his exercise. She found him infuriating that way. He had those freaky genes. He could eat whatever he wanted and stay all long limbed and slender. Susannah ran because it helped with the panic, yes, but also because she thought if she didn't, her ass would bloom like a roasted onion.

"Yeah, trail running," said Max. "David goes out and runs for hours on these trails in the woods. Sounds like something Freddy would love."

"Fuck that," Freddy said.

"Hey, language," Susannah said.

"Yes, language," Max said. "Though I do think curse words are undervalued. I mean, *fuck* is like the English-word equivalent of Eskimos having so many words for snow. Tremendous versatility."

She smacked Max on the arm. "You're not helping."

Freddy laughed, enjoying this breach.

All along she stared at Max, until the moment she saw him staring back. His blue eyes were icy water. They no longer danced and were no longer filled with the mirth of the moment. What Susannah saw in them was chilling. She saw in them what she'd seen that night many years ago on a New York street, when he punched a stranger and knocked him to the pavement. She saw the raw power of that time, as if his mask had been ripped off, and again it both frightened and oddly thrilled her.

Max doesn't run, she thought. *Yet he is going running with David Hammer.* Max never did things just to make friends, unless it served a larger purpose. Which could only mean one thing: he had lied to her the other night when he told her David Hammer couldn't be the one leaving the notes. Max still thought he was. What was Max planning to do?

Now he was shutting her out, too, and she had to do her best to pretend she had no idea about any of it.

It was raining that Saturday morning, rainy and cool. It had rained all night and a mist had rolled in off the lake and engulfed their neighborhood on the hill. Promptly at ten, though, David Hammer pulled up in his black MINI Cooper and Max jogged out of the house in shorts and a T-shirt and a Windbreaker and folded himself into the passenger seat of the small car.

David Hammer looked him up and down. "We need to get you a new pair of running shoes. Those aren't going to cut it for long."

Max looked down at his vintage Nikes and David was right: they were more stylish than functional, but then again, Max thought, only assholes, his beautiful wife excepted, ran. This wasn't about to be a new hobby of his. But Max was enjoying David's snobbery about this and all things, that smug look of superiority he had, that educated-white-artist sense he had that everything was open to being curated, from clothes to his precious little car, which was so immaculate inside it might as well have just rolled out of the showroom.

What a prick, thought Max.

They made small talk as they drove through mild traffic up and over the hump of Main Street, past the university with all the students waiting in packs to cross at the lights. Soon they were on the highway, heading south. The rain picked up and David had no music on and for a while they drove in silence, the steady scraping of the wipers a percussive sound track in the background. David drove cautiously, a hair over the speed limit, and car after car streamed by them in the left lane.

Fifteen minutes later they turned off on the Richmond exit and then onto a two-lane rural highway. They drove for about a mile, past the Round Church, so-named because of its shape, though it was actually an octagon, squared off on each side.

Just past there, David took a left and then turned onto a dirt road that took them up a steep, forested hill. At the top of the hill, the woods gave way to open fields and a sprawling old brick farmhouse, with falling-down small barns behind it, one of them leaning so precariously it looked as if it might collapse just from the sound of David's tires on the wet dirt road.

Soon they were back in the woods and climbing on a dirt road so pocked that Max thought David's precious car was going to bottom out. The road went from two lanes to one, and the forest, mostly spruce, came right to the edge of the road.

Just as they were about to crest a hill, David pulled into a small turnoff, an old logging road, and carefully nosed his car in so that it wasn't sticking out. "This is it."

They climbed out into the rain. They stepped onto the trail and David stopped and faced Max and began to stretch, windmilling his arms in fast circles, leaning forward on one knee and then the other. Max followed suit and they did this for a few minutes and David said, "You ready?"

"Born ready." Max smiled.

David broke into a run and Max followed.

At first the pace was easy, a jog, and Max thought this wasn't so bad, but soon they were going straight up a hill, jumping over rocks and fallen logs, and Max's lungs started to burn but he wasn't going to let David know that. The forest was lush with spring and heavy with rain. Giant ferns grew everywhere, and when they reached the top of the hill, the trees parting in front of them, Max could see down to a steep ravine below. David stopped and Max, breathing heavily, did, too.

"You okay, old man?"

"Fine," Max said.

Now that they were standing still, the blackflies descended upon them, small swarms of them that they swatted at. They were all over Max's head, the back of his neck.

"That's why we have to keep running," David said, and he took off down the hill, darting between trees, and Max followed.

Max struggled to keep up, and for a time David was decently below him, his head appearing and bobbing and then disappearing before reappearing again. Everyone hunted deer where Max grew up. Since he was without a father, Max did not. He had never hunted or even fired a gun, other than a BB gun when he was twelve and he and his buddy, Todd, used to try to shoot crows out of trees and blow out streetlamps in the small village.

But this was what Max imagined it was like to have a whitetail in your sights, bouncing below you, trying to get free so you couldn't squeeze off a shot.

This thought inspired him to push past the pain in his lungs, and he was soon hurtling downhill and caught up to a smiling David, where he stood overlooking a massive gorge, carved rock on either side, a steep drop-off, and down below, looking over the edge, Max could see a churning spring river. David wasn't even breathing hard.

"What is this place?"

"That's Huntington Gorge. You mean you've never been?"

"No."

"Crazy place. Not sure you want to swim down there, though."

"Why's that?"

"You'll see when we get down there. There's a waterfall. It causes crazy currents, especially when the water is high. People get sucked under and drown. Mostly high school kids, jumping off the rocks. All kinds of warnings posted, too. And even a sign with the names of those who died."

"Damn," Max said. "Well, we won't swim but I'm curious to see it now."

David started to run again. The trail widened as they moved downhill and soon it leveled and now Max could see the river clearly, fast moving and muddy.

They left the tree line and now there was the noise of the falls, to their left, falling into a wide pool, rushing down into a series of pools, the water gray and white and churning. Above, a sheer, wet wall of granite extended up to where they had come from.

"Pretty cool, huh?" David said.

"It is."

"Just can't swim in it. Though lots of people do."

Max nodded. The rain falling felt good, cool and wet against the heat of the run he had done. He watched the water, and over near the waterfall he saw a long stick moving through the currents, getting stuck in a vicious vortex for a minute, trying to fight its way downstream but unable to, before eventually breaking free and crashing against the rocks.

DAVID DROPPED MAX OFF SOMETIME after noon. Every part of his body ached. It hurt as it had not in a long time. Susannah was out food shopping and Freddy was at a friend's house. Max took a hot shower, and in the shower he kept picturing that falls and the water and he thought, *What a fucking gift.*

On their way out, David and Max had stopped and looked at the green sign that had the names and dates of all those who had died in that spot. Innocent kids, the lot of them. Unlike David Hammer, Max thought, who had made the bad choice to try to mess with Max's family.

An empty house is a beautiful thing. The rain had picked up again and he heard the sound of it on the roof. He went naked to his bed and fell on it, slung half the comforter over his bare legs, and fell asleep.

SUSANNAH WOKE HIM UP. SHE woke him by climbing on top of him, straddling him, and leaning down and kissing his forehead. Max came to with her red hair hanging in his face and said groggily, "Hey, love."

"Freddy is home, downstairs."

"So?"

"You need me to be quiet." She reached her hand down and fondled his cock.

Max rose for her, as he always did, and with his hand gently over her mouth she moved on top of him until he saw the fragility in her face, that moment of letting go where she disappeared into herself, her eyes blank as the sky, leaving the room for a moment before coming crashing back in.

She collapsed on him. Max rolled her over. They lay together, looking at the ceiling.

"What did you do to David Hammer?"

Max laughed. "More like what did he do to me? I can barely feel my legs."

"You didn't hurt him?"

Max leaned up on his elbows and turned toward her. "No, why would I hurt him?"

"I saw the look in your eye at dinner. You forget how well I know you. You told me he wasn't the one doing this to us, but I didn't believe you. And I don't blame you for lying. I know you were just trying to protect us—me and Freddy."

Max looked down at his wife. He looked at her big beautiful eyes, and her gorgeous skin, the thing that above all else defines beauty in women when they get older. He looked at her lush full lips, and he wanted to tell her, he really did.

He wanted to share all of it with her, as a husband and wife should. Max wanted nothing more than to lay it all out for her, in great detail. But she was fundamentally right: he was protecting her and Freddy.

"Some things are better if you don't know."

Her eyes flashed. "That's patronizing."

"No, no, it's just smart. Not that anything is going to happen. But if it ever did, you know? I mean, what if you were given a lie detector test or something?"

He said this on purpose. Susannah was scared to death of machines, anything vaguely hospital-like. She couldn't have her blood pressure taken. It made her feel constricted, and Max seriously doubted that anyone would be strapping her to a lie detector, as if this were the CIA or something, but they had both seen the movies.

Her features softened. "I love you."

"I love you, too. Always."

"At least there wasn't a second note. I live in fear of it. Every day I think I'm going to go for my run and find it out there."

"There's nothing to worry about, okay?" Max said.

"I just want you to be careful. Safe. All of us."

"Shhhh. Really. Trust me. Have I ever let you down?"

"Maybe a few times?" She smirked.

"Never." He rolled over on top of her. "My turn to do the work."

Susannah looked up at him with those crazy big eyes and took his hand and playfully brought it down to cover her mouth.

HER HUSBAND WAS A LIAR. Max had always been mercurial—sometimes brooding and difficult, but Susannah expected that. He had an artistic temperament. What the world saw of him was all light and charisma and that smile that could light up the winter. In private, though, he had moments of darkness. But in all their years together, she had never caught him in a lie. When they were first together, Susannah used to worry about other women. Not that there was anything specific, but she knew how women responded to him because she had. It was more her insecurity, she knew. Sometimes back in those days they would be out at a bar and a beautiful girl would walk by, all sashaying T and A, and Susannah would see her and look at Max thinking, *He's going to peek and that's normal,* but he never did. His eyes never wavered off Susannah.

She had never wanted to be one of those women who went through her man's phone. She had never done it. There was never any reason to. She felt his desire like you felt the breeze. They had ups and downs, some fights, and they weren't perfect. But they never stopped having regular, and passionate, sex.

Her friend Rose used to say all relationships ended the same way. "You no longer want to fuck each other, Susannah. Then you resent the other person, find fault, and then trust goes. You see devils around every corner. The paranoia begins to swallow you whole. And you are done."

No, that wasn't an issue for them.

Oh, how Susannah wanted to call Rose and let her know all about this. Susannah wanted to vent and tell her that Max had lied to her, have Rose tell her it was a big deal, that every little lie mattered, and give Susannah the chance to defend her strong husband.

But she knew she could not. She had a deep sense of foreboding about how this was going to play out. It was eating her up. What did that second note say?

Whatever it was, it was enough to get Max out on a run through the woods. It was enough for him to lie to her. And maybe his intentions for both of these were entirely good, but Susannah could feel the bad to come, as if something momentous were waiting over the next hill in front of them and no matter how quickly they swerved, they were still going to hit it.

THAT NIGHT AT DINNER THE joke was how much that run had kicked Max's ass, what an old man he was. Freddy got a kick out of it, Susannah pretended to, but she was going through the motions, keeping her head in the conversation, even though all she could feel was the panic under the ice of her skin.

She had made scampi, sautéing shrimp in butter and garlic and parsley, and dumping them over angel-hair pasta. It was one of Freddy's favorites, and her two boys ate with relish. Susannah drank white wine. More than she usually did. Like lots of people with anxiety, Susannah had a love/hate relationship with alcohol.

Oh, how beautiful it could make you feel in the moment. But overdo it and the next day you were much more likely to have the panic come on like a flood. But that night she didn't care—she wanted to be a little drunk. She wanted to be high, she wanted to quiet the nagging voices and sedate herself.

Max went upstairs early and took a bath. Freddy went to his room and closed the door and she knew he was playing one of his video games, headphones on, connecting with people around the world with the same interests, which mostly consisted of pretending to be mercenaries, gangbangers, and car thieves.

She cleaned the kitchen, finished off the bottle of wine she had started, and though she knew she was definitely going to pay for it tomorrow, she liked the way it made her feel. She suddenly wanted to dance and had this pang of memory of being younger and going out to clubs in New York. When she was with her girlfriends and a favorite song would come on. How they all recognized it from the opening beat and rose up as one to go to the dance floor.

She remembered what it was like to live like that—how carefree she once was with her body, how it felt to move without thinking, the time before she became aware of every tiny sensation and thought it meant certain death. Sometimes it was hard to remember that there was a time before when she lived in fear of losing her mind.

When the kitchen was clean, she drifted upstairs. She stopped outside Freddy's closed door for a moment and listened. She knocked softly. He didn't answer, so she tried the door and it opened.

To her surprise, he was asleep on his bed and fully clothed, his comforter to the side of his curled-up body. She walked over to him, pushed his hair to the side, and kissed him gently on the forehead. He stirred for a moment but did not wake. She pulled the comforter over him and left the room.

She went to the bedroom she shared with Max. He was asleep, too, under the covers, his mouth slightly open, and all the lights were on. Susannah considered climbing into bed with him but she wasn't tired.

What was wrong with these two? She was up before both of them and maybe it was just the wine, but the night felt young to her.

She thought brightly about smoking a cigarette. She was pleasantly drunk now. She returned downstairs, and in the kitchen she fetched her pack of American Spirits from above the refrigerator and went out to her spot, through the back door and under the eaves.

The rain had stopped and the night air was sweet like flowers. To her left, the moon, a day away from being full, had just cleared the evergreen trees in the neighbor's yard. The moon was hazy with clouds. She lit her cigarette and inhaled deeply. God, she loved smoking. She knew it was the worst thing in the world for her, but she loved the feel of the slender cigarette in her fingers, the lit tip, the taking of the cloud of smoke into her mouth and down her throat.

"Mostly," Joseph used to say to her in session, "you like it for the control: the taming of fire in your hand. It's an ancient impulse. It's also the world's most perfect antidepressant. So it's no surprise you enjoy it, Susannah. Even though it is the poor man's suicide."

She hated sometimes how Joseph came to her uninvited, his words like talismans, so that every action she committed there he was, long dead, having something to say. Sometimes she wished he would stop narrating her life, trying to define her from the grave.

She smoked greedily and looked at the moon. The moon was fat and hazy as she began to walk. The grass was wet under her sneakers and all around her the air was warm and moist. Winter took forever here to lift, but spring came on like thunder.

Susannah walked through the cut in the hedges and then around the front of the house to the street. The neighborhood was whisper quiet, though in the distance she heard the crawl of cars going down Main Street. The only lights were from the streetlamps, which glowed yellowish in the hazy night, and the grand old Victorian houses were hulking and dark. The rain that had fallen earlier was puddled in places on the asphalt.

She didn't have a plan. She just walked down the sleeping street, deeper into the neighborhood and away from town. She walked past house after house, in the most exclusive neighborhood in Burlington. She didn't know who lived in them, with a few exceptions, but she knew they were university people—professors or administrators— and some executives from places such as IBM, which had a corporate campus nearby.

The moon was her guide and she walked toward it, taking a left at the end of the block and climbing up the small hilly street, mar-veling at that grayish-white orb above the trees in the starless sky.

She found the fox on the side of the road. She almost didn't see it. She almost walked right past it. But out of the corner of her eye she saw this shadowy form lying on the ground, and when she went to it, she saw that it was a small red fox that must have been hit by a car.

Susannah bent down and took out her phone and scrolled up to the flashlight and turned it on.

He was on his back, his head lolled to one side, dead. He was lean and beautiful with long threads for whiskers and brown marble eyes and his fur was the deepest red except for his belly, which was the color of straw. If he were not lying on the side of the road, she would not have surmised that a car had killed him. He looked unmarked. She reached down and touched him, first his shoulder, then his spindly legs, and his belly. To her surprise, he was not cold, and when she petted his belly, it was slightly warm to the touch.

Susannah turned off the light on her phone and slid the phone into her back pocket. She put her hand under the fox's head and her other hand under his back and picked him up like a baby. She stood slowly and brought him to her chest, and through her shirt she could feel the sharp click of his dead claws.

WALKING BACK HOME, SHE HELD him to her chest like a stray kitten she had found. One car rolled down the street and past and the headlights lit her up for a moment before going beyond and taking a right and heading down the hill.

In the kitchen, Susannah laid the fox on the big round cutting board. She laid him on his back and he slumped slightly to the side and now in the light she saw how beautiful he truly was, the long whiskers and the thick red fur and those soft, sentient brown eyes.

He must not have been dead long, for he was warm and limber in her hands. When she was a child, Susannah's father would sometimes go upstate where a friend of his from Spain had decamped from Queens when he retired. Her father and his friend would spend the weekend trapping rabbits, as they had done in the old country. When her father returned home with two or three rabbits, he would present them to her mother as if they were necklaces, holding them up by the legs so she could see how they hung fat and long.

Susannah's mother's eyes would light up with this gift, as they did at Christmas when every year he bought her a new Lanz nightgown.

Her mother would take the rabbits into the kitchen and open them up below the neck, deftly disemboweling them with her strong hands, removing the organs and cleaning the insides under cold water. She did the same with fish he caught at this point on the East River.

Now, holding a sharp slender knife, Susannah almost instinctively crossed herself. She wasn't religious anymore, but in moments like this, she still believed in being present with the sacred.

She opened the fox from stem to stern. She reached in and took all his warmth into her fingers. This was an act of love, she thought, a bringing back of life.

She cleaned him and washed him carefully in the sink, bathing him like a newborn.

In a few days, Susannah would take him in a shoe box to a place in the northeast kingdom of Vermont, where a taxidermist would finish him, stuff him like a toy, and return him to her, and she would keep him in a box in her closet, under a pile of sweaters, hidden like a secret.

To Max, Saturday seemed both far away and ridiculously close. That week went by like a blur, classes and office hours, a lecture he gave at a nearby half-ass college barely even registering as something to remember, his voice in a big room echoing out like some lounge singer doing it by rote and no one giving a shit because they recognize the song. They all rose to their feet when he finished. Afterward, a line of students and faculty waited to talk to him when he came down the stairs from the stage.

It was all so fucking easy sometimes, Max thought.

At home Susannah seemed strong to him, the latest darkness having lifted. That Thursday, he decided to take her out, a last-minute date night. It was another beautiful and warm late-spring evening. They ate at Leunig's, a busy bistro down on Church Street, and they sat outside and drank a bottle of red wine and slurped oysters and ate steak frites and watched the people walk by and listened to a young couple busking.

He was on the fiddle and she sang and at their feet was a mangy pit bull. Behind them were their oversize backpacks, everything they owned. Their clothes were tattered and their hair long and scraggly and dreadlocked. They were crusty punks, as Max once was. Max looked at the boy's pants, cut off at the knees, his beard that didn't grow full, the dirt caked onto his calves, and Max tried to remember himself back then, before he shed that life like a snake sheds its skin.

But he couldn't. Over the years the layers had grown too thick.

When they were leaving, Max and Susannah stopped in front of the buskers, and they were quite good. The boy's playing was strong and her voice, though high and reedy, had this great Southern inflection that made the hairs stand up on the back of Max's neck. From his wallet Max peeled out two twenty-dollar bills and held them in the air so the boy's eyes, small and brown, could see them before Max theatrically dropped them into the fiddle case. The boy gave Max a huge tobacco-stained grin.

"That's generous," Susannah said.

"I don't mind paying for art."

MAX SAW DAVID HAMMER ONLY once that week—in the hallway outside their offices. David's was about three doors down from Max's on the third floor of that old brick building. Max was going out as David was coming in, and right when they ran into each other, Max's phone began to buzz and he looked down to see a Manhattan number he did not recognize. Manhattan, the Western center of the art world, was usually good news and Max wanted to answer it, but there was David, wearing his usual button-down and jeans and Chuck Taylor sneakers with no laces.

Max looked again at his phone.

"Hey, Max. Up for more punishment Saturday?"

"You bet. . . . Sorry, I need to take this."

"Pick you up at nine," David said, brushing past Max and into his office with its wide view of the quad, whereas Max, being the new guy, despite his appointment, stared out at the parking lot.

"See you then." Max then walked, answering the phone.

"Max W?"

"This is him."

The voice on the other end was calling from Goldman Sachs, the Wall Street giant. Would Max be willing to come give his "You Are the Art" talk to their employees at the annual meeting this June? He had come to their attention, the man said, when his TED Talk of the same name went viral a few years before. Goldman was interested in having its traders think about their work as art, as much as science.

The enemy, Max thought, and this was precisely the type of thing that would barbecue one in the art world. "I'm rather busy."

"We'll pay you fifty thousand dollars."

"You got my attention. Why me?"

"Good. We've been impressed with what we are hearing about you. And we usually bring in someone out of the box, not what you might expect Wall Street types to listen to at an annual meeting."

"That's by design. I don't allow videotaping or the use of phones, though. It's meant to be a live experience."

"Understood. By the way, Bon Jovi has the same condition."

"Bon Jovi?"

"Yes, the band. They are going on after you."

"Amazing." Max couldn't help but laugh. From homeless to opening up for Bon Jovi, hair rockers who do stadium shows, and on Wall Street, of all places.

America can be a bright, beautiful place some days.

IT WAS WARM AND THE sunlight dappled through the trees and onto the trail as they finished stretching and set off on the same run they had done the week before. David led and Max followed and the deer run they were on was bone-dry now, hardened dirt, and David went fast moving up the steep hill.

They did not run together—Max could tell David Hammer enjoyed this part, the competitiveness of it, as if he were putting Max in his place somehow, proving that David was the fitter of the two of them, as if that mattered a whit to Max.

When they reached the top of the hill, Max's chest was on fire, the breaths coming in pants, and this was the spot where they had stopped last week, but this time David did not so much as pause and instead plunged down the trail and Max followed. His knees burned with the downhill. The air was thick and still and the blackflies were out again and he smacked at them as he ran.

Once again, David broke away from Max, the white of his baseball hat moving between trees far below. Max ran as hard as he could, aware of the pounding of his legs on the hard dirt, stepping over fallen logs, swiping at the cloud of tiny flies around his head.

Max came out of the tree line and onto the rocky floor of the gorge. David stood near the edge of the pool, his hands on his hips. Max stopped running. Now that the pounding in his ears slowed, he could hear the raging water to his left where it fell ten feet in a torrent over the rocks.

David turned his head to watch Max walk toward him.

"You all right, old man?"

Max shook his head. "Barely."

Max walked until they stood side by side. David Hammer was looking down into the water. Under his tight T-shirt Max could see the rise and fall of David's breath, the intake in, the shape of his ribs, and then the long exhale out.

They watched the rock-lined deep pool and the falls and the water that swirled violently in circles.

David half turned his face to take in Max's. "You never went to CalArts, did you?"

Once, while on the road, Max watched a small guy beat the shit out of a bigger guy outside the bus station in Philadelphia because the bigger guy had tried to sell the small guy a dime bag of oregano. It didn't seem as if he should have been able to take the bigger guy, and Max knew both of them vaguely from traveling, so another night he asked the small guy how he did it. Always hit first, he said. And don't stop.

David turned his head away from Max then, toward the falls. He was waiting for Max to answer. Max smashed into him like a linebacker, his shoulder low and aiming for his ribs.

"What the fuck?" David Hammer said as he fell into the water.

His head poked above the churning foam. Max watched as the current moved him swiftly away from Max in an arc and toward the falls. Only a hell of a strong current could move a man as if he weighed nothing. As David started to swim against it, Max jumped in after him.

The water was freezing cold. It took Max like an undertow but on the surface. He spun almost halfway around, heading toward the center of the pool before moving almost into David Hammer's arms. It was like water ballet, the two of them, a delicate and serious dance.

"What the fuck is wrong with you?"

But Max only smiled at David, Max's biggest smile, the one he reserved for the end of a talk, when the crowd rose like a single organism, one loud thundering clap that filled the room, applause that he lived for, the moment when it engulfed him like an avalanche.

The current brought them together as if in an embrace. *It's stunning*, Max thought, *when a man is going to die and has no idea*. David Hammer's eyes widened, his arms came up, and on his face was a look of complete puzzlement as Max rose up in the water and wrapped his arm around David's head and locked him tightly to him and took him under the water.

David knew the score now. He thrashed like a fish and was strong. His fingers were in Max's face, his nails scratched furiously at him, but Max pushed down as hard as he could until he felt David go limp, then let go.

Max bobbed and gasped for breath as he watched David Hammer surface and float away from him and under the falls where the water pounded his flaccid body.

MAX WAS RUNNING ON ADRENALINE. Near the falls the currents were even stronger and he sensed the tumble of it everywhere, wanting to take his body and pull him down to the depths the way he had pulled David Hammer down, until Max was spinning as if he were in a washing machine and couldn't get out.

David was floating on his stomach as Max drifted toward him. Max watched David's legs swish back and forth, as if he was alive and building momentum to hurl his body toward the rocky face under the waterfall.

Max kicked his legs to close in and suddenly it was like turbulence in an airplane when your stomach drops from the urgent loss of altitude. Max was under, under David, on his back, fighting to climb back up, but it was as if he were hooked to a rope at the bottom of the pool. He kicked as hard as he could.

He came up spitting water, shaking the water from his head at the moment David barreled into him, solid as concrete, and then it was as if the entire weight of the waterfall, a winter's worth of snowmelt, were pounding on his head and shoulders. The sound was deafening. Max shot under again, and he thought, *This is the manner of my death. It ends here*.

His head smashed into rock. That was the last thing he remembered.

THE FIRST THING MAX HEARD WAS the sound of water, lapping against him. He was beached like a canoe, half on a flat sliver of rock, half in six inches of stream. He blinked and opened his eyes. A searing pain was on the left side of his head. When he put his hand up there and brought it back down, Max saw the crimson red of his own blood sliding down his fingers.

He pulled himself out of the water and sat up. Now he remembered getting sucked under, hitting his head. Looking up, he saw the falls straight ahead and off in the distance from where he sat.

Somehow, unconscious, he had floated out of the pool and then down the slope of shallow stream to here, maybe fifteen feet from the mouth of the stone pool. How was he even alive?

The flies were all over him like a piece of carrion. A dark swarm of them, tiny, were landing on his face, especially on where he was cut. He tried not to think about this.

Max managed to get to his feet, swatting at the blackflies with one hand, while holding his aching head with the other. He had a moment of vertigo and thought he might go down, but somehow he willed himself to stay upright.

The pool they had been in was slightly uphill from where Max stood now, and he began to walk slowly along the side of the rocky stream back toward it. As he rose up with the land, he saw David Hammer, stuck near the mouth of the pool, his body lodged against a rock ledge, his legs moving obscenely back and forth in the current. It was a miracle that Max had made it out and down to where he could breathe.

Max needed to get David out. The water, the current, the current that had almost killed Max, scared him and he moved gingerly around the rocks, stepping over the small stream to the other side, where David Hammer lay facedown.

Max bent down and took David's hands in his and began to pull on David's arms. Max pulled David until he could lean down and put his hands under David's armpits, then he tugged hard to get him out of the water.

Max fell backward onto the bank and David Hammer fell down on top of him.

Max slid out from under him and stood up. Max was out of gas, breathing hard again. But David's eyes were open and Max didn't know what he expected, but it wasn't to see those vacant blue eyes. David's glasses were gone, somewhere in the pool probably. On his neck were the scratches from Max's fingernails. This didn't surprise Max, and he knew they would raise questions, but the answer was easy, wasn't it? He had tried to save him. That was what happened. He fell in, and Max tried to save him and almost killed himself.

Max left David Hammer on the rocks. He followed the route they had run only an hour ago back up the hill, through the woods, climbing the ridge to where on the other side, in the lee of the trees, sat David's car.

Max moved slowly, his body broken and his head soupy, one foot in front of the other. When he touched his head, his fingers came down still covered in fresh blood. It was hot now and he wondered if he had a fever.

While Max didn't want to know what he looked like, he knew this was a gift. When help arrived it would appear he had been through the wringer, too, which could only add gravitas to his story. It was a tragedy on a spring day, so terrible, but nobody's fault.

Somehow he made it to the car. He opened the door and took his phone out of the bag on the passenger-side floor. The words he was about to say were going to be the most important words he had said in a lifetime of saying words. They would be recorded and they would be assessed. Nothing mattered more than how he sounded.

Max forced himself to cry. He imagined that it was Susannah's body on that rocky riverbank and that she was gone forever. The tears came and stuffed up his nose.

He leaned against the hood of that small car and dialed 911.

"There's been an accident," Max said, when the operator came on. "My friend drowned. I'm really hurt. Hurt bad."

"Sir, where are you?"

"A dirt road. I don't know the name. We were at Huntington Gorge. Oh, God . . ."

"Stay on the line, okay? Stay with me. We are sending help now."

Max stayed on the line. "Okay," he said through tears.

The blackflies consumed him. He knew it would be a while. But he stood and listened for the wail of sirens and the scramble of tires coming up the hill.

THAT MORNING, BEFORE THE PHONE call came, Susannah felt oddly calm. She watched Max bound out the door to David Hammer's waiting car, and after they left, it was almost as if she could feel Max running through those woods, as if she were doing it herself in a dream, the strain of his quad muscles, then the feel of the icy river water when he plunged in after David. Sometimes they were symbiotic like this—two minds connected by an invisible thread. Maybe that's why she was calm. She was calm because Max was. He knew what he was doing.

It was a beautiful morning. She dragged Freddy to the farmers' market downtown. He didn't want to be there, or at least with her, for he was of the age now when everything Susannah did embarrassed him.

"You need sunlight," she said to him.

"Mom, I'm fine."

"You're going."

A Saturday morning Vermont farmers' market is a thing of beauty. Susannah could not go there without being reminded of her mother, and the wistful stories she told when Susannah was a child about the markets in Madrid, which her mother had missed about Spain more than anything else, teeming with fresh vegetables and fish that had been trucked in from the sea. While there were no fish at the market in Burlington, it had newly plucked vegetables and meat and eggs from local farms and gorgeous breads. Susannah had made a commitment to herself to try to shop here every week, to bring home a bounty and then fashion meals all week for Freddy and Max. It would be her challenge, her labor of love: cook fresh and healthy out of the breadbasket that was Vermont.

The market was bustling. Sometimes crowds bothered Susannah, but not this kind, with the wide-open air and families with children and dogs and street performers everywhere. Freddy vanished on her almost immediately. At the north end of the market, some kids from school were break-dancing on a piece of cardboard, and he skateboarded over there as if he didn't know her at all.

It was early in the season. Too early for the sweet ripe summer tomatoes, but not for pencil-thin local asparagus and greens, and Susannah bought some of both. From a vendor, an elderly dark-skinned woman, who had a sign that said FREE HUGS, Susannah bought some lamb-leg steaks and some ground beef.

Her final stop was at the local bread company, where the young guy with the long goatee flirted with her, as he had at the end of last summer. Susannah didn't know if he remembered her or if he flirted with everyone, but the way he looked at her brought a smile to her face.

Susannah's phone started to vibrate in her back pocket. She didn't get it in time, but it was a local number and she thought, *Oh, well*, but then they called right back.

"Hello?"

"Susannah Garcia?"

"Yes?"

"This is Officer Brisbane from the Burlington Police Department. There has been an accident."

THERE ARE MOMENTS WHEN TIME stops. Moments when all around you things move in slow motion and the fog you fear is not fog at all, but profound clarifying numbness, and thank God for the body that continues to move when all you want to do is shut down.

Susannah ran through the crowd with her bags flapping against her legs toward where Freddy did skateboard tricks off the curb next to white kids popping and locking to hip-hop on a former refrigerator box they had opened flat and laid out on the cobblestones. She grabbed him frantically by the shoulders and, when he tried to brush her off, said, "Max was hurt, we have to go. He's in the hospital."

She didn't even remember driving. Somehow they ran to the car, got in, and sped up the hill to the university hospital.

Susannah felt as if she were swimming through soup after she parked the car and they went in through the emergency entrance. She never liked hospitals. The glare of the lights, the click of shoes on linoleum, the antiseptic smells, and most of all the sense that no one, outside of the staff, chose to be there.

They hadn't told her much on the phone. Just that Max was here and that he was stable. She had tried to say that over and over in her head. *Stable*. It was a good word and she didn't know the whole range of words but she knew enough to know that it didn't mean "critical."

The nurse looked him up on the computer. "He's not ready to see you yet, but it shouldn't be long. They're just finishing up."

"Finishing up? What do you mean?"

"He's going to be fine. He took a pretty good blow to the head, some loss of blood. He has a concussion. They're just stitching him up now. But if you want to take a seat, I will let you know."

Susannah was grateful to her. She was an older woman with streaked-gray hair and a kind face. She didn't talk to Susannah in jargon—*The doctors are reassured* or some such thing. The nurse said simply that he was going to be fine. Thank you.

Susannah and Freddy sat down on the hard plastic seats that were joined together. It was like waiting for a bus. Freddy looked bored and Susannah realized that she hadn't spoken to him since they got in the car, and he must have seen the tightness in her face and didn't want to pierce the bubble she was in.

She reached over and put her hand on his knee. "You okay, honey?"

"Can I walk home? It's not far."

"No, Max is going to want to see you. It won't be long."

Freddy slumped in his chair, his hair falling over his eyes.

It was almost forty-five minutes before they were brought upstairs in the elevator to the fourth floor, where Max lay in a bed in a small room. He was hooked to an IV and on his head a bandage protruded out as large as a softball and came right to the edge of his blue eyes. On the left side of his bed, a young nurse with a high ponytail and blue scrubs looked up from where she was scribbling on a clipboard.

"Oh, Max," Susannah said, going over to the right side of the bed next to him, Freddy trailing behind her.

"I'm fine."

"Did he hit you?"

Max looked at her sharply and then over toward the nurse. "What?

No, of course not. Why would he hit me? It was an accident. David fell in. I tried to save him."

"What do you mean 'tried to save him'?"

"They didn't tell you? David Hammer drowned."

Max came home that night with instructions to take it easy for a few days. No bright lights and lots of rest, he was told. The state police didn't believe this precluded them from visiting, which two did, both in uniform, a man and a woman. On the street outside the house, all three local television stations had stationed their satellite trucks, two of them sad small vans with a dish on top, and the other one looking new and like a small RV.

Susannah drew the blinds down and Freddy disappeared into his room to play video games. Susannah had wanted to stay and listen to what the cops had to ask Max, but they asked if they could be alone, and that they might have questions for her afterward.

Before they came, and after Max was settled in upstairs, he told her what had happened. He was groggy and his eyes were slightly glassy but his words were pure Max, clear and forceful and she almost believed them. She wanted to believe him, even, but she knew differently. Though for the moment she felt that she had no choice but to play the dutiful wife.

"He just slipped," Max told her slowly. "It was crazy. He got there first, to the gorge, and I was maybe two minutes behind him running down the hill. David was standing with his back to me, looking over at the falls. I remember he turned toward me, like he was about to say something. Next thing I know he's falling backward into the water. At first I laughed. But then I realized he was in trouble. I sprinted over and went in after him. The current was insane. I was trying to pull him out but he kept getting sucked under. He was clawing at me for help. Then I hit my head. I have no idea how long I was out. When I came to, I was so lucky. Somehow I had gone downstream. David was floating on his face in the pool."

"Oh, Max. Max."

"It's going to be a zoo, Susannah. For a few weeks. For all of us. The press will be knocking at the door. It's important we don't say anything yet. When I am able, I will talk to them. But I don't want you and Freddy to have to, okay? This happened to me."

"It sounds like it happened to David."

"Of course, yes, it did. I feel terrible for Joanie. I mean, we made fun of them. But they were perfect for each other."

Susannah sighed. "It's going to be huge at the university."

"Yes, it is. Listen to me. I know you won't like this. But until I am well enough to make a statement, hopefully tomorrow, I need you to stay inside, okay? Backyard should be fine. But don't go out front. There will be a lot of interest."

She nodded. She looked into his blue eyes, which though hazier than usual were still that icy blue, both warm and unknowing at the same time.

"I got it, Max."

"Thank you." He looked at Susannah as if she were a student he had just taken a conference with, and now she was dismissed.

"ANGER SEPARATE FROM HUMAN EXPERIENCE, from human feeling and empathy," Joseph once told her in therapy, "can grow like a weed until it consumes you. But few of us truly hate, Susannah, when you get right down to it. Sociopathic behavior, put simply, is the absence of empathy. I want you to try something for me."

"Okay."

"This is a game."

"I don't like games, Joseph."

He sat back in his leather chair, stroked his chin thoughtfully. "Indulge me."

"I don't like indulging you."

"You don't have a choice."

She glared at him but didn't say anything.

"I want you to imagine a dungeon."

"No."

"Yes, Susannah, a dungeon. Picture it. It's dark and damp and subterranean. Metal bars. Stone walls. No windows. Close your eyes for me. Can you see it?"

"Yes."

"What do you see?"

"I see dark rock walls. They are uneven. Slick with water. It looks very old."

"Yes. What else do you see?"

"Nothing, Joseph. I see nothing."

"Good. Now here is what we do. I want you to imagine someone you hate. Someone who has done you wrong. And here's the thing, Susannah, the big thing about this. You get to torture them."

"Torture them?"

"Yes, however you want. Pick your weapons. In fact, I want you to imagine them. What is in that cell? Are there razors? A hammer? A knife? You get to choose." Joseph paused. "But there is one important caveat to this whole fantasy. Well, actually two. First, you have to look them in the eyes when you hurt them. You have to see the hurt in their eyes. And you are not allowed to look away, do you understand?"

"Yes," she whispered.

"And the second caveat is equally important."

"Okay."

"There is a reset button for them. They get to press it. And when they do, the pain goes away, whatever harm you have inflicted is reversed, but they remember that you did it. Do you understand?"

"Yes."

"So who do you want to hurt, Susannah?"

"Nobody, Joseph. I don't want to hurt anyone."

"What about your father? He gives you up just because you fall in love?"

She shook her head. "I love my father."

"Your mother? She didn't defend you. She shrank away and let you go. The very woman who birthed you?"

"No, no, no."

"Your sister?"

"Stop it. I don't like this at all."

"Do you want to hurt me, Susannah?"

"Of course not, Joseph. I'm not playing this anymore."

Joseph sat back in his chair, stroked his chin again. He looked at her, then past her shoulder to the bookcases behind her. "Time's up."

Max's head hurt and even the wan late-afternoon light coming through the window was way too bright and his eyes did not want to be open. After Susannah left, he closed them to conserve his energy—he knew the crucible to come—and he fell into a deep sleep.

He dreamed that he was running through the forest, as he had been earlier in the day. Those sunlight-dappled woods were lush and green and he moved effortlessly, his body a machine, legs and arms pumping up the steep hill. In front of him, he saw the figure running in the distance, coming into view for a moment before disappearing around a bend in the trees. Max picked up the pace—he needed to catch him. It suddenly occurred to Max where he was going. He was going to the car, and he intended to leave Max behind, out in the middle of nowhere on a dirt road. He would drive to the police station up near the lake and tell them what Max had tried to do.

Max ran faster. He was so fast. He burst up the hillside and he felt no burn in his lungs—he was a child again and he could run forever.

He was gaining on him. He popped into sight at the top of the hill, the white of his shirt, and he was no more than fifty yards away now. Max crested the rise and then the slight downhill in front of him, and there he was, moving toward the trailhead. Max picked up the pace yet again, practically sprinting, and when he got within twenty yards, he yelled, "Stop."

And he did. He stopped. He stopped and turned around to face Max.

It was no longer David Hammer. Instead, Max's mother stood there, and she had aged, her face heavily lined, her hair streaked with gray, but still wearing that baby-blue eye shadow she loved. She was smoking one of those generic cigarettes, holding the crumpled pack in the claw of her other hand.

"Phil, is that you? You look so grown-up."

"No. No. No. No."

"Phil, come home." A pleading was in her voice. "It's been forever."

Two state troopers stood at the entrance to his bedroom, a man and a woman. Max saw them instantly, assessing him, and he thought, *These must be the two who wanted to see me at the hospital*, with the nurse running interference and saying unless it was an absolute emergency, it should wait until later.

He must have still looked jacked up, because before they introduced themselves, the female trooper said, "Are you sure you can talk? We could come back."

"I'm okay." Max mostly was, though the dream lingered, just beyond his grasp, as if the concussion had knocked something from the past loose in his head. It had been years since he had thought of his mother.

He was tall and out of central casting for a state trooper, broad shouldered and with the clichéd superhero cleft chin. His name was Loftus. She was stout and wide hipped, but she had a pretty face, with dark eyes and full lips. Her name was Scott, though she looked Hispanic, and while they were both in uniform, she said they were detectives with the state police. She did all the talking, and by the way Loftus looked at her, his body language, Max could tell she was the senior officer.

She moved over to the side of his bed, while Loftus stayed unmoving at the foot of it, as if he were ready in case Max made some kind of run for it.

"Do you mind if I sit down?" Detective Scott said.

"Please."

She sat down on the edge of the bed. "How are you feeling?"

"I've had better days."

She smiled. "I bet."

"It's all very surreal."

"Oh? What is?"

"How your life can change in an instant."

"Tell me about that."

Max shrugged. "It hasn't sunk in."

"You're still in shock," she said softly.

"Yes, I suppose so."

"How did your life change?"

Detective Scott had kind eyes. Max sensed she was probably excellent at her job, for looking into her dark eyes he found himself almost wanting to tell her all of it, starting with that night in the Adirondacks when he became Max W. She had that way about her.

"One minute it's a beautiful day. The next moment your friend falls and he's fighting for his life."

"That what happened? He fell?"

"Fell? Slipped? I don't know. I was pretty far away."

"Were you good friends?"

"No, I barely knew him. We were colleagues. We had just started hanging out, really."

She nodded at this. "You said 'your friend.' But you taught together?"

"In the same department."

"But you ran together?"

"It was our second time. It was something he did all the time. Trail running. I was new to it. He invited me."

"So tell me everything you remember."

Max walked her through it, as he had Susannah, though he started earlier, with how they were starting to become friends, that they seemed to have a lot in common, that David and his lovely wife had come to dinner and there they had talked about running and David was so passionate about it that Max became curious about this idea. Then David invited him and this was their second run together. David chose the spot and was familiar with it and Max had never been there before and didn't know Vermont well.

As he relayed the events of that morning, their run, how far ahead David was, his turning toward Max, then falling into the water, Max's attempts to get him out, how strong the current was, like nothing Max had ever before experienced, he was even more pleased with the strength of this story. It was threadless. It was one giant piece of cloth.

When Max finished, Detective Scott turned to Detective Loftus. "Anything I should have asked that I didn't?"

"I don't think so."

"Oh, one more thing. I think they will do an autopsy and all that. But he had some serious marks around his neck. Lots of scratches. Any idea why?"

"There wasn't much to hold on to," Max said. "That pool was like a fast, swirling drain. I was grabbing on to whatever I could to try to get him out. At one point, it was only his head above water. I probably got his neck."

Detective Scott nodded. "Makes sense. I don't know if we will, but if we have other questions, you will be around? No travel coming up?"

Max remembered the Goldman talk. "Nothing this week. But I have a speech in New York next month."

"A speech? Are you a politician?"

They both laughed.

"No, no. I give talks on art."

"Of course, I didn't mean anything by it."

"It's okay. I suppose us academics deserve it."

"I'm terribly sorry for your loss."

"Thank you."

AFTER THEY LEFT, SUSANNAH CAME in and Max could tell she was running hot. He knew her too well. She was doing her best to hide it, but the giveaway, as she sat on the side of the bed and asked him if he was hungry, was her hands. In her lap, she was kneading them together over and over, all her fear visible in those slender fingers that were turning red from her effort.

"Not yet. I'm going to talk to the cameras."

"Wait, no, why?"

"Because they won't go away until I do. Don't worry. It'll be okay."

"What did the police say?"

"They just wanted to know what happened."

"What kind of things did they ask?"

"Just that. Listen, it was a hard day. But this is okay. A terrible thing happened. Sometimes terrible things happen. It was an accident, okay? An accident. We'll get through this."

Susannah nodded but looked as if she might hyperventilate.

"One more thing," Max said. "Do you have a number for Joanie Hammer? I think I should call her. I only have David's in my phone."

"I don't."

"Can you try to find it?" Max wanted to give Susannah a job, something to focus on.

"Sure."

Twenty minutes later, still wearing his running clothes, but barefoot and with a big bandage on the side of his head, Max emerged outside the front door. As soon as the door opened, people rushed toward him from the three satellite trucks, cameramen with the cameras on their shoulders following coiffed anchor-types coming across the lawn. Max stepped onto the porch so that they were below him. The two men and one woman each looked around twenty-five years old, and he could see in their faces and the way they held themselves that they were pale imitations of their national counterparts, but that they dreamed of bigger markets. Max knew something about that.

Max stood there and let them come to him. He knew he looked like shit. He looked exactly like a man who had almost drowned, which was precisely the optics the moment demanded.

The camera lights went on and were in his eyes. Questions were shouted that he ignored.

He spoke and they went quiet.

"I want to ask for privacy for me and my family. Our thoughts and prayers are with all those who loved David Hammer. He was a brilliant artist and a great teacher. It is a very sad day. I want everyone in the UVM community to know—"

Max choked up. He felt his voice break and he stopped talking for a moment. Max looked down, away from the bright lights and the eager faces in front of him. He covered his face with his hands and sobbed.

Max lifted his face back up. He took his hand away and let the tears flow.

"I did everything I could to try to save him. I wish I had done more—though I don't know what that might have been. I am new to Vermont. But that is a very dangerous place: that gorge. When a fit, healthy man can simply fall into water and die, no one should swim there ever. Thank you."

They shouted questions. But Max tried not to hear them and instead turned and opened the door and disappeared inside and closed it behind him, moving first toward Freddy and ruffling his hair before moving past him. Max took his wife into his arms, brought her fast-ticking heart next to his, and whispered into her ear, "It's over now."

THE DAYS THAT FOLLOWED WERE the blurriest days of Susannah's life. It was as if the death of David Hammer were a giant forest fire, consuming all the oxygen for miles around. After Max gave his remarks on the front steps of their house, the press disappeared from their front stoop, though the phone calls continued. No one answered the phone. But, thankfully, the police didn't come back.

On Tuesday, there was a vigil on the great lawn at the university, and hundreds and hundreds of people came out, a sea of lit candles. They walked up together as a family. Max had asked to say a few words, and a makeshift stage was in front of one of the red stone buildings. The university president, a large man with an impressive head of black hair, spoke first. For a president, he wasn't a gifted speaker. His words were obviously written for him and came out stilted, but Susannah barely listened anyway. She was focused on Joanie Hammer, standing behind him. She looked so tight. Her face had a look of panic Susannah recognized, as if the mask had been taken off Joanie and underneath was just a raw tangle of fear.

Sometimes Susannah saw a similar look on her own face, in photographs that others had taken when she was unaware of the camera, times when she was at a party and lost in her thoughts, oblivious that what she projected was pure, unadulterated tension.

On the big lawn, Freddy saw some friends of his and disappeared into the crowd.

Max had left her, too, and was now stage right, waiting to be called. Susannah found herself drifting backward, away from the stage and deeper into the crowd. She realized she was afraid of being seen as the wife of the man who had been with David that day. She didn't know why this scared her—maybe it was simply the size of the crowd and not wanting eyes on her. If she was asked, she wondered if she would deny it, like Simon Peter from her Catholic childhood.

After the president finished, Max's boss, Ernst Werner, the chair of the art department, spoke. He was short and had to pull the microphone down to his face. His German accent was thick and clipped. He told a story about the first time he saw David Hammer, how he couldn't believe this man was the artist he had heard about, someone who was making waves with the ephemeral art he did. Instead, Ernst said, David looked like an accountant from some white-shoe firm. This got a laugh. Then Ernst talked about the teacher David was, how he always had extra time for his students, what a natural he was in the classroom. A selfless, wonderful man. Especially, Ernst said, his voice choking up, when it came to the love of his life, Joanie.

Ernst turned and looked toward her. "He was a model to many of us for how to live and love."

Ernst turned around and stepped back.

Max came to the microphone, his head still bandaged. Susannah stepped backward and into the darker shadow of a maple tree, leaned against it and looked across the quad to the stage where her husband's strong face was framed in light.

"Hello, everyone." Max adjusted the microphone back up toward him. Susannah felt a stir in the crowd at the sound of his voice, as if everyone all at once leaned forward into his words. The power that Max had from a stage, the place he was most at home.

For a moment, Max just stood there, taking everyone in. He had told her once, "Audiences are patient, Susannah, they want you to be slow with them, bring them into your embrace. No matter how big the room, your job is to make it intimate. It's not a hard trick, but few do it well."

When he began to talk again, he surprised Susannah by telling the story of David's final hours. It didn't seem appropriate, but she could tell people were riveted. The only sound was Max's voice booming out into the night and the sound of cars moving slowly down Main Street.

"We were in the woods. The air was thick and stifling. The flies were terrible, all over us. But David loved it. He loved every moment of it. He was an unbelievable runner. He moved like a deer through those woods and in that heat. He was a half mile in front of me and there was no way I could keep up with him."

Suddenly, someone was next to Susannah. She turned and on her left was the state cop, the woman. Susannah didn't remember her name and almost didn't recognize her, since she wasn't in uniform.

As if sensing this, the trooper said, "Detective Scott."

"I remember."

"He has a way with words, your husband."

"David Hammer died the way he chose to live," Max intoned from the stage.

Susannah nodded. "Yes, he does."

"I can't say I knew him well," Max said. "And many of you know this, but academia can be a hard place to make friends." Knowing chuckles came from the crowd. "But David lent me his hand in friendship. He reached out and said, 'Welcome.' We broke bread together, David and Joanie, and me and my wife, Susannah. I should have done more that day. I should have fought harder. I can't help but believe that if the situation were reversed, if I was the one that fell, David would have saved me. I have to live with that the rest of my life. But, Joanie: I cannot fathom the depth of your sorrow. I am so sorry."

Max stopped talking but didn't leave the podium. He stood there, much as he had done on the stoop of his house in front of the cameras and put his head in his hands. Susannah could not hear him cry but his shoulders shook. Everyone was still and everyone was quiet. Next to Susannah, Detective Scott said nothing.

Then Joanie came up to him from behind, and as if sensing her, Max turned, and he took her in his arms, and for the longest time they just hugged, her face in his shoulder.

Somewhere in the crowd, someone started to clap, then everyone was, the sound of hands clapping growing louder and louder, and for what felt like forever, it didn't end, the most sustained ovation of Max's life.

Joanie did not speak. The university chaplain closed out the vigil with a prayer, people putting their heads down.

When he finished, Detective Scott turned to Susannah again. "Your husband, did he study theater?"

"No, he's an artist, why?"

The trooper looked at her in the dark and snuffed out her candle. "Seems like something he'd be good at, don't you think?"

"I have to find my son." Susannah turned away from her.

"Susannah." Susannah stopped. The detective moved toward her, and Susannah braced herself instinctively, but what Scott did was hand her a card. "Call me if you ever want to talk."

"Why would I want to talk?"

"You feel safe at home?"

"Of course. What kind of question is that?"

"One we're supposed to ask." Scott shrugged. "But you do look like a woman with a story to tell."

"I'm not good at stories." Susannah put the card in the front pocket of her jeans and turned her back to the trooper and walked toward where she had watched Freddy disappear an hour ago.

A PART OF SUSANNAH DESPERATELY wanted to believe the story that Max had told her, the story that he told to the television cameras at their front door, that he told to the hundreds who gathered in the warm spring night in the shadow of those grand old academic buildings.

She wanted to believe that it was an accident, that David Hammer lost his footing and slipped. But Susannah had seen the look on Max's face that night they ate out on their porch with the Hammers, and she kept remembering something he had told her when he moved from making his word paintings to giving his talks:

"The power of a story is in repetition. It's iterative. If you say something enough times, and say it with authority, you will be believed. It's all in the delivery and in being consistent. Do that, and an audience will lick the words out of your hands like they are their own."

The memorial service was that Friday at the Ira Allen Chapel on campus. The morning of it, she went for her run. The air was cool and the skies were leaden and gray and it looked like rain. A breeze was blowing off the lake, and as she came down and past it, it looked like the ocean in winter, wide and gray and covered with whitecaps.

As she ran, Susannah kept seeing in her mind David Hammer standing on the rocky riverbank, sweat glistening from the run, looking at Max, who had come down the hill breathing hard. Does Max go for his neck first? Or does he push him in and follow him in after?

On the path along the lake, Susannah stopped running. She stood with her hands on her hips looking out at the water. The ferry was on its way in from Plattsburgh, but otherwise the lake was devoid of boats. On sunny days, the whole stretch toward the mountains was peppered with sailboats, like something out of Matisse. But today, it was just gray.

She stood there looking out and feeling the breeze push her hair away from her face. The funny thing was, she thought, that sometimes—perhaps because you were in love, and make no mistake, she loved this man, really loved him—you could float on the surface of things and not see the dark depths in front of you. As she stood on that walkway, other runners going by and kids like Freddy zooming on their skateboards, it sank in her belly like a stone that her husband had killed another man, another living, breathing human being. Max had snuffed him out of the world as easily as if he were a candle blown out at the end of a vigil.

That first note suddenly seemed like a lifetime ago. But the words were still raw and fresh.

I know who you are.

And this was the thing Susannah knew about panic, about the white bear: sometimes it clouded your judgment so that you could never see what was in front of you. Back when she read the note, she knew that it was creepy, that it was meant for them, and that it felt menacing, a violation of their new home. It never occurred to her, until now, that it might be specific. A bell went off in her head.

"How well do you know him, Susannah?" Rose had said that day at the Standard Grill, so long ago now, in the city life Susannah once led.

Susannah had dismissed the question, since she believed she saw the contours of his heart, and when you know those, is there anything else that really matters?

They were both just orphans in the world when they met, weren't they?

But then again, what if David Hammer knew something about Max from the time before? The art world was a small place. She remembered David on their porch asking Max about CalArts, though she was so blurry with anxiety that night that she couldn't remember how he answered any of it. Max didn't like to talk about the past, which was hardly a crime, though he had a philosophical answer to this as well. Talking about the future was far more interesting, he said.

"Nobody cares who you were," he said in his talks. "They care who you wish to become. The caterpillar becomes a butterfly. The world doesn't stop. But it pays attention, for a fleeting moment, to the new beat of wings."

Maybe David Hammer cared, Susannah thought. Maybe he found out something about Max that he never wanted anyone else to know, not even her. Betrayals come in both big and small forms.

Susannah started to run again. She was headed away from their house, following the shore of the lake north. For a bit she ran as fast as she could, as if she could exorcise these dark thoughts from her mind if only her legs pumped fast enough.

THE MEMORIAL SERVICE WAS PACKED. Susannah pleaded with Max on the way there to sit in the back. She was worried about the crowd, feeling them close in around her, but he was insistent that it was only appropriate that they move up to the front. As they walked down the aisle, Susannah heard the whispering, a distant Greek chorus, as everyone, all at once, seemed to recognize Max. *That's him, the one that was there that day. That's Max W, the famous artist that everyone is talking about.*

Though she couldn't hear a single word, just a murmur that went through the grand old chapel as they moved past.

They settled into the third row, and at least, Susannah thought, they were on the aisle. Freddy didn't come. Max tried to reason with him, it was an important rite of passage, something to mark, etc.— but Freddy said, "Look, I didn't know the dude."

Susannah let it go. She couldn't fight with a teenager. Not today.

The ceremony was a fog, and an odd replay of the vigil on the green, many of the same speakers, sans Max. After the minister spoke, a beautiful reed-thin older woman rose and walked up to the pulpit. It was David Hammer's mother.

With a rich Southern accent she began to talk about her son. Susannah wouldn't remember her exact words, but at one point she stopped, then her elegant voice cracked as she said, "The cruelest thing in the world is burying your child."

When she said that, Susannah lost it. Max put his hand on her back as the tears came forcefully. For the first time that day, Susannah was fully present, looking up at the pained face of a woman she did not know behind the pulpit, hearing the voice of one mother who could have spoken for all mothers with those words.

A FEW DAYS LATER, MAX returned to his office to find Detective Scott waiting for him in the hallway. He saw her first. She was reading the bulletin board across from his office while she waited, the way all the students did, the posters announcing speakers and vigils and the like, though she was in her trooper uniform, her elaborate hat tucked under one arm.

Max took a deep breath and then let it go before she sensed him. She turned to him, and as he walked toward her, he smiled.

"Sorry to show up unannounced."

"Not a problem." Max swept his hand toward his door. "Please, come in."

They went into his small office. Max closed the door behind them. He dropped his messenger bag on top of his desk and motioned to the chairs in front of it and she went to one and sat down. He went behind his desk and sat in his chair, as if it were just another office-hours meeting. Detective Scott was taking in the room. The bookcase with the smattering of art and art-theory books, the photo on top of it of Susannah taken on a Manhattan street in winter, her red hair cascading to her shoulders and her eyes bright against the snowy day. The word painting he had done of her years ago above it on the wall, the only one he had ever kept, the word FERAL in bold caps slicing across the middle of the white canvas and through other words written smaller and in different scripts.

Detective Scott was pretty but severe looking. Her curly black hair was tight to her head and held back by a hair clip at the base of her neck. But her eyes were deep and intense, and now they looked up at Max and he wondered where this was headed.

"I could have called, but I thought it would be better to talk in person."

"I'm glad you came by."

"Are you?" She looked at him quizzically.

"Yes. Phones can be impersonal, don't you think?" Max tapped his fingers lightly on the desk before correcting himself.

"I'll jump to it. The state's coroner has ruled the death an accidental drowning."

Max peered at her. "Did you expect something different?"

"The drowning part doesn't surprise me. The accidental is somewhat subjective."

"I don't know what you're suggesting."

She shrugged. "It doesn't really matter. The good news for you is that the state's attorney considers this matter closed."

Max smiled at her. "You sound disappointed, Detective. By the way, what is your first name? *Detective* seems so impersonal."

"Dolores."

"Dolores. I like that."

"Why?"

"It's old-fashioned. Not a name you hear anymore."

"My Puerto Rican mother liked it. It means 'sorrows.'"

"Sounds like you're in the right line of work."

"Anyway, I am not disappointed, to answer your first question. I just wonder—"

"What?"

"A very fit, very athletic young man just slips. Standing on a rock and he just slips. Doesn't make a ton of sense, does it?"

"It was wet."

Detective Scott shook her head. "I've stood on that rock when it's wet. Wearing shoes like this." She lifted up her foot to show him her shiny black shoes, smooth soled on the bottom. "Mr. Hammer was wearing running shoes with good traction. I didn't feel that it was slippery at all."

"I was twenty yards away at least. So I just saw him fall. I didn't see what led up to it. But it sounds like there is something you want to say, so just say it. We're both grown-ups here."

The detective sighed and stared at Max for a long moment before turning her gaze to the wall, and he watched as her eyes moved up to the canvas full of words.

"Is that yours?"

"Yes, early work. I don't paint anything anymore."

"Tell me about it."

"I turned the idea of life modeling on its head. Rather than see form and classical shape, I saw emotion. I did that with Susannah modeling for me, back when we first met. She took off her clothes and lay nude on my couch and I walked around her for an hour and didn't filter my thoughts—just wrote down what came to me as I studied her. Later, I put them on canvas. Nothing too complicated. Only requires a beautiful woman to disrobe for you."

"I imagine that was never difficult for you."

"Do you find me persuasive, Dolores?" Max saw her brace a bit at his use of the familiar.

"Doesn't matter what I think. Clearly you are good at what you do. Anyway, I won't take any more of your time. As I said, you can consider this matter closed."

Max nodded and watched her stand. "It's never closed, though, is it? I mean, just because you say so. I have to live with what I saw for the rest of my life. What I failed to do."

"Right. There's that. Have a good rest of the day."

Max watched her walk toward the door. "You can leave it open."

She stepped out into the hallway and was gone. He went to the window of his office, which overlooked the parking lot. A moment later he saw her emerge from the back door and he watched her walk across the parking lot to her car, which he could tell was a cruiser even though it was unmarked, the big antenna pointing up off the roof a giveaway for anyone who had ever spent time on the streets. It was a narcmobile, Max thought, the language coming back to him as if it had never left.

"Are you going to look up?" Max said audibly under his breath. "If you look up, you're not done with this, even if the state says you're supposed to be."

She reached the car, put her hand on the door handle, then stopped. Max watched as her eyes ran up the side of the building, taking in the windows until she reached his.

THAT NIGHT THEY WERE IN the kitchen and Susannah was cooking and Max was sitting at the island with a glass of wine when he told her Detective Scott had come to see him. Susannah felt her breath catch in her throat but Max continued. What he said was mostly a blur but the long and short of it was that the autopsy had come in, and they had ruled the death accidental, and not suspicious. David Hammer had died from drowning. There would be no more investigation or need to talk to Max.

Susannah studied his face when he told her this. He was a practiced liar, she now knew, and he was acting casually about the whole thing, as if he had just gotten news that his class schedule had been rearranged, or as if he were talking to a receptionist setting up a dentist's appointment for a cleaning.

But all through dinner and then after, Susannah felt an energy coming off him that she had not seen in a long time. He was electric, Max was, a bundle of kinetic energy. She saw it in his eyes, and in his hands across from her at dinner, the clench and release, the three of them eating enchiladas as if they were any American family on a weeknight, talking about work and school and looking at the planner on the wall filled in with a Sharpie with the week's coming events.

As soon as Freddy disappeared, Max did the dishes. Susannah was standing at the counter when he dried his hands on a cloth and came up behind her. He slid his arms under her and leaned down and his mouth was suddenly on her neck and she felt him hard under his jeans and against her ass.

"Oh, really?" Susannah said.

"Oh, yes."

"Freddy could walk in."

"Freddy is knee-deep in an alternative world upstairs."

Max knew how to get her going. "The garage?" she said.

"What am I?"

"The mechanic who fixed my car and I couldn't pay the bill."

"How we going to resolve this problem of ours?" Max said in that working-class New York accent. It never got old for her.

"Stop it," she said jokingly, in a tone that showed she didn't mean it.

"Never."

They moved into the garage, locking the door with the dead bolt behind her. Max bent her over the hood of the Volkswagen, lifted her skirt, and when he pushed inside her, there was that urgency, his hands rough as he held her hips. Sometimes men just needed to fuck, Susannah knew. They needed to let it out, not just the release either, but the whole thing. The feeling of being inside a woman, taking her, the ownership that can come when you agree how and why you let yourself go.

Afterward and upstairs, they showered and he was gentle with her, this man that she should have been afraid of. He massaged her shoulders while the water ran over both of them. He reached around her and held her by the belly, his fingers over the scars she wore from Freddy that he called beautiful. All scars tell a story. He whispered that he loved her. Susannah kicked her head back and moved into him over and over.

But later, after he fell asleep, Susannah was restless. Max slept like the dead some nights. She felt alone, even though he was there, and suddenly a deep, inexplicable pang of loneliness swept over her. She looked at the clock. It was eleven-thirty.

Susannah climbed out of bed and walked down the hallway to Freddy's room. Light was under the door. She stood outside for a minute, listening, and thought about how children become teenagers and they were like having a tenant. When do you impose yourself?

She knocked. "Freddy?" she said softly.

The door opened. He wore baggy shorts and a long T-shirt. "What's up?"

"You going to sleep?"

He shrugged. "Soon, I guess."

He didn't want to talk to her, and it saddened Susannah. It wasn't long ago that he was her shadow, and now he was swimming away from her, leaving the spawning grounds for the wide ocean, and it was part of growing up, she knew, but it still stung a little bit. Where did her little boy go?

"Okay." Susannah reached out and ruffled his hair. "Don't stay up too late."

"I won't." Freddy closed the door.

Susannah went downstairs. All the lights were off except for the light above the stove, the one next to the vent, and it cast a yellow glow out into the kitchen.

Max's laptop was sitting on top of the island. She opened it and it came to life and she typed in his password, *Susannahlovealways*, and it flickered to life. *This is trust,* she thought, knowing each other's password, *so why are you doing this?*

Susannah clicked on his browser and the Google screen was there and she typed in *Max W* and pages of results came up. Articles with headlines such as "Artist Makes Splash by Putting Words to Canvas" and "Radical Artist Max W on Why Making Things Is a Waste of Time."

Susannah had read all of these before, and now she scrolled past them. She moved down the page, to the next one, and she didn't know what she was looking for, but then she saw something that caught her eye:

"Area Family Has Not Given Up Hope in Finding Missing Son."

Susannah clicked on it. It was an article, four years old, from a South Carolina newspaper:

The family of Maxwell Westmoreland of Charleston hopes that their son is still alive and that someone may have knowledge of his whereabouts. Mr. Westmoreland was last seen at the family's vacation home in upstate New York though he is thought to have disappeared from New York City on or about June 13, 2005. Mr. Westmoreland lived in New York City and was working as an artist, according to the family spokesperson, Clifford Mayes. Prior to moving to New York, Mr. Westmoreland had graduated from the California Institute of the Arts, where he earned both a BFA and an MFA in painting.

The Westmoreland family is prominent, with roots deep in South Carolina. The missing man's grandfather is the late General William Westmoreland, who commanded US forces during the Vietnam War.

Susannah could barely breathe. She read the short piece again, then looked at the photo of the young man in it, and while there was a resemblance, it was clearly not her Max. But in her head were his words to her that very first night they met: "General Westmoreland was my grandfather."

Later he said he was joking and that he didn't even know who his grandfather was. He said that his grandfather was most likely some professional dirtbag living in a small western New York town. *Probably in jail like my dad*, Max said. *I come from a long line of winners.*

But why, in this case, did this missing man have the same name as her husband, why did he have the same degrees her husband had, and the famous grandfather her husband once joked was his before correcting it? And why did her Max always insist that his degrees never be publicly disclosed? Any bio of him anywhere never mentioned where he went to school.

"Let them think my education was the streets," he told her once. "And in reality they were. I learned more about art being homeless than I ever did at an expensive art school."

Her head swirled. She stared at the screen. She read that short article again and again as if by doing so it would somehow come into clear relief and Susannah would know what she was looking at.

She was so engrossed that she didn't sense Max coming up behind her. He put his hands on her shoulders and she practically jumped out of her skin.

By the time his fingers were on her skin, it was too late for her to close the laptop.

Susannah started to shake. Max leaned down next to her. His face rested on her shoulder, his breath was hot on her ear. She knew he was looking at what she had been looking at.

He spoke softly. "It's time for a talk, love."

MAX BROUGHT SUSANNAH OUTSIDE IN the dark. He led her by the hand. He took her through the kitchen and out into the backyard, down the steps and across the patio. They were barefoot and the grass was dewy on their feet. Max took her across to the far corner of the yard, where a wooden swing sat in front of the rows of peonies that separated their property from the one behind it.

They sat down on the swing, their feet anchoring it on the ground. They would not be swinging. It was as if Max, holding her hand, felt all of her in his fingers. He could sense that motor starting to run, as if she were a kite about to fly away from him if he didn't coax her back down to earth.

Susannah looked up at Max and it was light enough that he could see the shape of her features but not her eyes, which meant she couldn't see his eyes either.

"I need to tell you a story. A story you can never tell anyone."

"What did you do? I don't want to know."

"It's probably not what you're thinking. Please, Susannah, just listen, okay? It's not a bad story, I promise. It has a happy ending."

She was nodding but looking away from him toward the back of their house.

Over the years, Max had learned that a story can be told in many different ways, especially with a rapt audience. But when the stakes were high, such as at this moment, there were a couple of different schools of thought on how to proceed. Max decided to get the biggest shock out of the way first. Treat it like boot camp, in other words, break her down and then work, slowly, to build her back up.

"My name is not Max Westmoreland. Well, it is actually. But it wasn't always."

Her voice got hard. "What is your name?"

"Phil Wilbur. That's how I was born."

"What else have you fucking lied about?" she said loudly.

Her agitation was not just in her voice. She was starting to shake.

"Not so loud. Please. I was born Phil Wilbur. I never wanted to be Phil Wilbur. There is a grand tradition here, Susannah, which I am a part of. A grand tradition of art. Was Iggy Pop born Iggy Pop? David Bowie, David Bowie?"

"Oh, fuck you. You're not a rock star, you prick."

"You're right, I'm sorry. I don't even know how to tell you this!" Max said with enthusiasm. "Really, please. This is beautiful. Okay. Let me try.

"I ran away from home as a teenager and I lived on the streets. I traveled around and I studied the straight world from the shadows. I looked at it from cities where I sat on sidewalks and begged for money for food and booze. I slept outside."

"All this I know. At least that part you have told me."

"And it's all true. So I was thinking of leaving that life when I met a man. He was a few years older than me. He picked me up hitchhiking. His name was Max. He was an artist and a rich kid and he wanted out of his life, too. We became friends. He took me up to this house his family owned in the Adirondacks, this giant old summer place they had built on top of a mountain. We spent this long weekend hanging out. It was the first time I had slept in a bed in years. Max hated his family and he hated his name. He was gay and from this ultraconservative Southern military family. His grandfather, as you read, was General Westmoreland. Every male in his family going back a long way had been military officers. I don't know, but I related. I really believe sometimes we are born into the wrong identity and have to start over, ourselves, when we are old enough to do it.

"Anyway, we were hanging out, drinking out of the liquor cabinet and thawing steaks to grill, and my hair—I still had hair then—was a ratty dreadlocked mess and I asked Max, who kept his super-short, if he would cut it for me. When he did, we both freaked out a little because we suddenly looked like brothers. And then he had this idea."

"What?"

"That we switch. I become Max W and he becomes Phil Wilbur and escapes. And I was like, 'Why would I want to do that?' It sounded so crazy. And he told me he would give me ten grand to get started as him—well, not him, but his name and his identity to get me going, and something I lacked, both an undergraduate and graduate degree from a prestigious place. 'It's enough to get you a cool job in the art scene in New York,' he told me. I thought he was joking but I realized he needed this. And I did, too. A fresh start. And so we exchanged driver's licenses. We drove to the city together and he packed a bag and got on a bus for Alaska. And that's where he lives now. On this remote peninsula you can only get to by seaplane. He and the guy he fell in love with. They live completely off the land. And the rest of the story you know."

"You've talked to him?"

"Only once. It was a couple of years after we did it. He called to thank me. I was working in the gallery then. He tracked me down there. He told me he had fallen in love. He told me about his cabin that he had built on this remote land he had bought. How he could pull salmon after salmon right out of the river near him and smoke enough of them to last all winter. That he could finally be himself. That he was free for the first time."

Max stopped. They sat in silence, alone with the sound of the crickets. Max could almost see his words sinking in. He saw Susannah's body relax a little; she was still on guard, but coming down from the height of the tree she had climbed. He was pretty sure she wasn't about to jump anymore at least.

"Why didn't you ever tell me?"

"I wanted to, I really did. But I made a pact with him that I would never tell anyone. And he did the same for me. It was critical that we protect each other."

"I don't think of myself as anyone, Max. Or do I even call you that anymore?"

"Of course you do. It's my name. It's been my name. I'm so sorry, Susannah. Believe me, I wanted you to know this."

"I don't understand how his family didn't find out. Wouldn't they have traced you? Figured out you were using his name?"

"There are lots of people with the same name, of course. But, yes, it's been a danger. The only link is the transcripts, which I am careful about. I still use my old name when I need to, like on the paperwork for this job. I told university HR that Max W is just a stage name. They didn't say a word about it. I don't use his Social Security number."

"Wait, what does he do, then?"

"He doesn't work. Doesn't have to. And lives off the grid. He has no need for it. He wanted to disappear."

"We should go to bed. It's so late."

"Come here," said Max.

"I'm not ready."

"Come here."

He put his arm around her, brought her close. She fell into him, her head against his and her feet lifted up, and Max pushed off with his and for the first time that night and in the quiet dark of the neighborhood, they swung in the air like children.

THESE WERE THE TIMES THAT Max needed to be vigilant. When things got tight and they got close, he needed to run triage like an emergency-room nurse, assessing the dangers in front of him and laser-focusing his attention on those that presented the greatest threat.

David Hammer had exited the stage, after overplaying his hand. The police were out, though Max didn't like the way Detective Scott had tried to look right through him in his office, her implication that she knew everything anyway, and that if she stared hard enough with those big eyes, he would fold like a cheap tent and tell her all his secrets, confess as if it were his job. *Think again,* Max thought.

Susannah, though, strong and delicate Susannah, his love, those golden-brown eyes so filled with pain and history, as if all of Spain's sadness could be contained in an upward glance. Families that traced back through what horrors? War and diaspora and everything in between and who the fuck knew what else? Her gaze was never penetrating, but it could be the deepest, most soulful you ever saw.

She, the light of his life, his girl, his forever, Max needed to put back together like a finished puzzle that had been scattered across a wooden table.

His sitting on the swing that night, telling her a story that held enough of the truth to hold it together like glue, was the first step.

In the days after, though, and for this Max was grateful, life began to return to something approaching normal. Final exams were on, which didn't mean much to the art faculty, such as Max, other than that the end of the semester, some final critiques, and graduation and the long summer to follow were staring them in the face. Max was ready to turn the page.

That was the thing about academia at its best: it had a rhythm to it, a flow that followed the seasons, or life itself, Max guessed, if you thought about it deeply enough. Things began and then came to an end. They started over anew and you did it again. But the best part was that a year came to a close and you didn't have to look back. First, though, Max had another ten days or so to get through.

And to keep Susannah together in the meantime.

She wore her struggle on her face. That beautiful face of hers that in the best of times was smoother than her age should allow was suddenly tight, drawn, creased, and perplexed, the look of a woman you might pass on the street and if you considered her at all, it was only to wonder if she had somewhere to sleep that night.

There was no easy antidote to this, but the key, Max knew, was to learn from seasickness. If you focused too close, it got worse, but if you fixed on the horizon, you could steady yourself and find your legs.

So, as he had done before, Max made them a future. Freddy's last day of school was Friday, June 20. Max went online and booked a house for a week on Cape Cod, the first Saturday in July, a little cape that sat on bluffs above the ocean in Wellfleet.

He didn't tell Susannah before he did it, and it was nothing they had ever done before. When had they had the time, or the money, for a vacation?

They would be an American family, Max decided. Even more than they had been before. School would soon be out and they were going to the beach. Load up the wagon and go lie down a blanket on the sand and have a fucking picnic.

"I have a surprise," Max said one night at dinner that week.

Susannah perked up, but Freddy looked at him skeptically, his eyes saying, *Any surprise you are about to bring my way I am certain not to like.* Or maybe he just didn't want to take a break from the huge plate of chicken Parmesan he was shoveling into his mouth.

"Hang on." Max walked into the living room to get his laptop.

When he came back, he was theatrical about it, knowing that Susannah didn't like surprises, though she would love this. She loved the ocean. She and Freddy were both staring at Max as he opened the laptop. He took his time, sitting down next to them, but keeping the screen away while he brought up the listing.

One picture in particular he wanted them to see, an aerial shot, perhaps taken by a drone, of the house in its landscape, perched almost precariously on top of high dunes, the great blue Atlantic right below it.

Max found it and enlarged the photo so that it filled the screen.

"What's that?" Susannah said. "Beautiful."

"We go there first week in July. I rented that house for a week. On Cape Cod."

"You're kidding?" Susannah said cheerfully, though Max could tell it was forced. He had work to do. She leaned over and kissed him on the cheek.

"Do I have to go?"

"Freddy?" Susannah said. "Of course you do. It'll be so fun. The beach is right there, look."

"You can bring a friend if you want, buddy," Max said.

This brightened Freddy a bit.

"But no video games, not at the beach," Susannah said, and Max wanted to tell her just to let him be for a moment, that they could cross that bridge a little later. But she needed kindness from him right now, not corrections.

So they had something to look forward to. *Check*, Max thought.

The rest of that week and the next Max went through the motions of the end of the semester. He got his grades in, did some final critiques, and bade goodbye to the students he knew who were graduating.

Mostly, though, he kept a low profile. Everyone's eyes were on him wherever he went—*He's the one,* etc.—so Max just kept his head down and knew it would pass. All things do.

Two days before graduation, Max got an email from his department chair, Ernst, asking him to stop by Ernst's office. Ernst had never before written Max directly about anything. Ernst was a hands-off chairman who only intervened if he had to, and even then reluctantly. Max had this moment of trepidation when he read the email, and it occurred to him that maybe David Hammer had filled Ernst in on part of what he had found out, namely that Max didn't hold the degrees he had said he did. Ernst and David were close and had known each other a long time.

It would be ironic if this was how it came crashing down.

The building that housed the art department had no air-conditioning, and on some days the brick kept it relatively cool, but as Max walked up the curved wooden staircase to Ernst's office, the air felt close to him, more than close, as if it were closing in, and he thought that this was how Susannah felt when her motor started to go and her world began to shrink.

Ernst's office was in the far corner and encompassed the turret, which gave it big windows that looked down toward the town below and the lake beyond it. From the few times he had been in there, Max remembered that the views were stunning.

As he came down the hall, Max saw that the door was open. Max stopped before he reached it, took a deep breath, then came around and saw Ernst, looking small behind his desk, reading glasses on the end of his nose, studying papers in front of him. He would have looked like some kind of eyeshade accountant if the office weren't carefully designed. The midcentury-looking desk that he had made himself many years ago when he was a young art student, his layered paintings on the wall, scraped over and over until they looked like ancient abandoned walls.

Ernst looked up and saw Max in the doorway. Ernst raised his head and removed his glasses. "Max, come in, please. Get the door."

Max closed the door behind him and came in and took a seat in the one chair in front of the desk, a stool, low-slung and speckled with white paint. Max chuckled to himself at this. Ernst didn't really like people, or students, and certainly didn't want them to be comfortable.

"How are you?" Ernst said in his clipped German accent.

Max shrugged. "Fine," he said, wanting it over with. "Semester almost over."

"Yes, yes, it is. Thankfully."

Max cut to the chase. "You wanted to see me?"

"I have a favor to ask."

Max began to breathe.

"It's a bit unusual, since you're technically a visiting faculty, but I was touched by what you said at the service about David and I thought it might bring some closure—to use a terrible word—if you chaired the search for his replacement. I've run it by the others and there was great enthusiasm."

Max smiled. It was not the smile, big and wide, he did for crowds, but the smile he couldn't help. "I'd be honored."

"Well, good, good, thank you. It's settled then. Louise can help you with the details, putting together a committee, the announcement, those kinds of things."

"I'm on it."

"Well, perfect then."

It didn't feel hot anymore when Max walked out of the building into the near-summer day. He felt like celebrating. The elation he felt was almost manic, like on the day he sold his first word painting. *Yeah, I will happily lead your fucking search*, Max said to himself.

The lake below was wide and blue and infinite. Goldman Sachs was going to pay him fifty thousand dollars to talk for an hour. The summer was in front of them: a house on the Cape right around the corner and a chance to hit reset.

That night Max splurged on Susannah. They dropped Freddy off at a friend's house and then drove south down the lake to the Shelburne Inn, a magnificent mansion from the 1800s smack on the shore. They ate on the porch watching the sunset. They had filet mignon and potatoes Anna and split an expensive bottle of French red, with crème caramel for dessert.

The next morning Max slept in and the two of them left the house at the same time, Max heading to campus and Susannah off for her run.

On the door, as it was closing behind them, and before he could do anything about it, Susannah saw the note before he did. He wasn't able to stop her. She reached for it first.

Max had been terribly, terribly wrong. This wasn't over. Not even close.

THE
THIRD
NOTE

IT DANGLED FROM THE WOODEN door, held up by a thin strip of Scotch tape. Susannah was quicker to it than Max, and afterward she would think it was because she was in that moment worried that somehow he would keep it from her, not let her make her own judgments, as he had with the last one, which was as patronizing as fuck when you thought about it.

Not today, my husband.

She grabbed it from the door and just as quickly he was behind her, leaning over her shoulder. Susannah opened it.

I SAW YOU DO IT

Susannah looked back at Max, and in the moment before he realized she was staring at his face, he looked stricken, but then just as quickly the mask returned. *Oh, he is so good at that,* she thought.

"Who are you going to kill now?" Susannah said loudly.

Max grabbed her wrist, hard. Max had never grabbed her before. He had never been physical with her in that way. It hurt, his hand tight and twisting.

"Be quiet. Susannah, really."

He released her. They both stood there, looking up and down the street. The street was whisper quiet. They were the only ones out at the moment, and it was a regular morning. It might as well have been an abandoned movie set they stood on, a completely perfect and manicured vision of suburbia. Everything was perfect, and full of perfect people, except for the two of them, who looked the part, but were sliding backward into their true, deep imperfections, where they belonged. They were at a loss for words.

THE ONLY MAN SUSANNAH HAD ever been afraid of was her father. She wasn't afraid of him in a physical sense—he didn't hit her—but she was afraid of him for other reasons. He was short, her father, but he had this power over her that she both wanted to move into and away from. He had a strict and narrow way of looking at the world, and when it came to his daughters, he expected them to adhere to it and in his mind there was no room for error. He drew lines in the sands of life. If his daughters strayed and crossed them, he wouldn't hesitate to turn them off like a faucet. As he did to Susannah when she came home with a baby boy.

Susannah was never afraid of Joseph. Sometimes he pushed her further than she wanted to go, deeper into things, opening her mind like a piece of fruit and peering inside it. He did make her uncomfortable. He made her move into her own skin in ways she was unaccustomed to. But she also knew he was fragile, especially physically. As he got older, especially in those months before his heart gave, sometimes she thought she could have pushed him over with a breeze.

And until now, she had never been afraid of Max. Not when she saw him level a strange man with a punch on a street, or even when she became convinced he was going to kill David Hammer. Sounds so strange and facile, but that was how Susannah felt.

But then Max grabbed her wrist. Like her father, Susannah had lines, too, and this was one of them. The marks and the bruising on her sore wrist were evidence of his crossing. She found herself both angry and afraid. She looked at him differently now, as if it had dawned on her for the first time that not only was he capable of hurting people, but that he was capable of hurting her.

MAX HAD LET GO OF her wrist. "Don't do anything, okay? Just wait for me. I'm going to be late."

Once he was gone, Susannah was inside trying to tell herself to exhale, and she decided she needed to go for her run anyway, because if she didn't, she would obsess about what the note meant, who wrote it, what the person was going to do.

But as Susannah did her loop, running down the hill and along the lake, it felt as if every set of eyes were on her. Even the most innocuous of glances, not the leering ones, the ones from women, say, were burning right through her. As if everyone knew something except for her.

As she ran, in her mind she saw the grimace on Max's face as he took her wrist in his strong hand. It occurred to her that she had seen that look before: that night the Hammers were over for dinner and David brought up CalArts, and when Max thought no one was looking, he burned daggers through David's skull.

David was dead two weeks later. But his fate had been settled in that very moment. He asked the wrong question, which in hindsight must have been innocent. David didn't leave the notes, for if he had, they would have stopped coming.

"We are products of evolution, Susannah," Joseph used to tell her. "Humans are simultaneously complicated machines and also very simple ones. Strip us away to our essence and you will see we are still the ancient people we once were, alone on a barren African beach, motivated by food and procreation, but mostly, the desire just to stay alive. Deep in a part of your brain lies the reptile you once were. When the tiger comes out of the brush, or more apropos, when the white bear emerges from the woods, do you fight or do you run?"

By the time Susannah finished her run, she had that feeling that she was stepping outside her body, floating away from herself, from the incessant beating of her heart, a throbbing in her ears.

She tried to shower it away. She smoked in her spot under the eaves, looking at the leafy backyard. The panic grew and grew like a plant. And this one, Susannah couldn't stop. Soon it was as big and blooming inside her as the peonies pushing up against the house.

Upstairs, Susannah hastily threw things into a suitcase. As many clothes as she could fit. Shoes and underwear and pants and skirts and toiletries just all piled into the biggest suitcase she had.

She went into Freddy's room. His clothes were everywhere, and Susannah picked them up and smelled them. If they seemed clean, she stuffed them into a duffel bag. In the bathroom, she grabbed him a toothbrush and deodorant.

Twenty minutes later, Susannah buzzed herself into the high school, on the next-to-last day before the start of summer. At the principal's office, the receptionist in the large room looked at her with obvious alarm.

Susannah knew that it showed in her face, the shattered look of a woman who'd just discovered someone she loved had died, or that her husband might kill her.

Somehow she got out the needed words. She decided to go with a sick grandparent. Freddy needed to be pulled from school. His papa was dying, she said. It was just a matter of time.

A phone call was made to his classroom. A brief conversation Susannah didn't pay attention to. Behind the receptionist, she could see the principal himself, a tall man in his forties with a hipster haircut and reading glasses, looking at papers in his hands. His office was sad, she thought, with one of those iron-blue metal desks that seemed to exist only in public schools.

Then in front of Susannah was Freddy, with his backpack and his skateboard, looking at her with something that bordered on disgust. "What is it?"

"We can talk about it on the ride."

"What ride?"

Susannah had no patience for this now. "Let's just go, Freddy. Come on." And to the receptionist: "Thank you."

"Of course," she said, barely looking up.

"Where are we going?" Freddy said when they had left through the heavy doors, out onto the scoop of driveway in front of the school, then across the lawn toward the parking lot.

"We'll talk in the car, Freddy. Please."

She practically frog-marched Freddy to the car. He threw his skateboard and backpack into the backseat, and when he did, he saw the suitcases there. "Mom, seriously. What is this?"

Susannah ignored him until they were inside and she'd reversed out of the space, driving quickly out of the school grounds and heading toward downtown.

"We are going away for a while. It's not safe."

"What's not safe?"

"Our house."

"What the fuck are you talking about?"

"Freddy! Language."

"Well, you're acting like a crazy person."

"I need you, I need you just to do this with me right now, okay? Please."

"Why isn't it safe?"

"Max isn't safe, okay? He's not. He could hurt us."

"What? What happened? Did you get in a fight?"

"I need to focus," Susannah said.

"Did he hurt you?"

"No, he didn't. But I am worried. And my first responsibility is to you and me."

Freddy slumped in his seat. He looked out the window.

They drove in silence for a bit, toward downtown, where Susannah pulled into the parking lot of the bank. "Wait here."

Inside, Susannah waited her turn behind a small line until a teller opened up. She was a woman about Susannah's age, big glasses, heavy and lots of hair.

Susannah said that she wanted to close her account, that she was moving.

"Account number?"

Susannah gave it to her.

She clicked away on the keyboard in front of her. "Is Maxwell Westmoreland with you?"

"Right now?"

"Yes. There are two names on the account. Both of you need to be here to close it."

Susannah forced a tear. It fell out of her eye and down her cheek. She leaned forward and looked the woman in the eyes.

The woman looked up with a soft and kind face at Susannah. "Are you okay?"

"I'm leaving him. He beats me. And my son. I need to go today. I need to go right now. Can't I just close it?"

"I'm so sorry." Susannah could tell the woman meant it. "But I can't close it without him signing as well."

"I need the money. It's mine."

"Well, that's different. Hang on. Let me look." The woman's fingers clicked away again, took a pause, clicked again. "There's no limit on what you can withdraw, though. Other than fifty dollars you need to keep in the savings account."

"Oh. What's the balance?"

"Let me see." More clicking. "Looks like twenty-three thousand four hundred and sixty-two in savings. A little over six thousand in checking."

"Give me all of it." Susannah smiled at her conspiratorially. "Minus the fifty dollars."

"Bank check okay?"

"Cash."

It felt as if it took forever, but it was probably no more than fifteen minutes. The manager came out and supervised, a fat guy with an overly sculpted thin beard who kept looking at Susannah suspiciously as if this were illegal, but when they finished counting, she was out the door with close to thirty thousand dollars in cash in fat stacks of envelopes. It wasn't all their money. Whenever Max sold something, he put it into securities. They might have a few hundred thousand there, but Susannah had never paid attention to it.

So Freddy wouldn't see it, when she reached the car she opened the back door and took the stack of envelopes, more money than she had ever thought possible for one person to have at once, and slid them into the mouth of her bag that rested on the backseat and pressed it closed.

Freddy looked at her wearily when she climbed into the car. "What are we doing?"

"I told you, we're going away for a while."

"Where?"

"I don't know. Freddy, please. No questions for now, okay, baby? I need to concentrate."

Under his breath he muttered something. Susannah heard the words "fucking" and "crazy" and she let it go. She wasn't a natural driver and she needed to focus.

"Just let me drive."

Freddy glared at her but didn't say anything. He took his earphones out of his backpack and slid them onto his ears, then Susannah heard the steady thump of the bass and he closed his eyes and looked toward the window and she gripped the wheel tight and led them out of town.

Susannah didn't have a plan—other than a nonplan to drive as far as she could away from Burlington and from Max. She went south on Route 7, following the shores of Champlain, past the rolling green of Shelburne and the small city of Vergennes, visible across fields in the distance. She deliberately chose not to get on the interstate because of some kind of misguided paranoia, imagining Max figuring out they were gone, borrowing a car or, more dramatically, jacking one from an unsuspecting student, pushing his way into the driver's seat at a red light and pursuing them at high speed down I-89.

So she drove. The farther they got away from Max, the better Susannah started to feel, and soon she was breathing, deeply and normally, in a way that made her realize that she had probably not done so for hours. Freddy was lost in the world of his headphones and it occurred to her—the mom part of herself rising to the surface—that he was probably hungry and that she herself hadn't eaten since breakfast.

"Are you hungry?"

Freddy lifted one ear on his earphones. "What?"

"Are you hungry?"

He shrugged.

When they reached Middlebury, she stopped at a small sandwich place that had a big OPEN sign on the side of the road, and when Freddy didn't want to come in, Susannah went and got them both sandwiches, a hummus-and-veggie one for her, and a roast beef for him.

They ate in silence as she drove, Freddy drinking a bottle of root beer, and Susannah water. The road was pretty. It was Vermont in summer, lush and endlessly green, mountains sometimes visible to either side, the Greens on their left, and the Adirondacks blue-gray rising up beyond the opposite shore of the lake.

At a gas station outside Manchester, they stopped to pee and Susannah thought of the money. It was more money than she had ever had on her before. But it suddenly made her sad because even though it was so much money, it was also finite. There was an end to it. Eventually it would run out, but maybe it was enough to get them started.

Susannah had begun again before; she knew how to begin again. She hated to toss and turn poor Freddy when it seemed as if they had finally landed. But she remembered the burn of her wrist after Max let go, and what choice did she have?

Coming out of the bathroom, Susannah took her phone out of her purse. Max had been blowing her up for the last hour. Seven new texts: *Where are u? You and Freddy somewhere? Is your phone off? Shouldn't Freddy be home? ???????*

Susannah looked over at Freddy, Snapchatting away on his phone. "Turn off your phone."

"Why?"

"Just turn it off."

"You're acting cray cray."

Susannah pleaded with him. "Please, Freddy. Max isn't who you think he is. And phones can be tracked. He could find us if we have our phones on. Look, I am shutting mine off."

Freddy rolled his eyes at her but did what she asked.

They moved through the afternoon and down the highway as if it were a river leading to New York. She could have gone west, she could have gone east, and she could have gone north, to Montreal maybe. But like a migratory bird, Susannah only ever went in one direction, back toward the only city she had ever truly known. She could get lost in New York.

For the first time in a long time Susannah had pangs that she didn't know she could feel anymore: a longing for her parents, for childhood, for the smell of her mother's cooking and a shared bed with her sister. She even missed her gruff father with his narrow views, his Old World Catholicism, and his paranoia about America. She didn't even know if they were alive, or if anyone would have told her if they weren't. But in that moment she wanted to go back to a time when she didn't have to make any decisions, but just did what she was told.

IN THE EARLY EVENING SHE stopped aside the highway near Watertown, Connecticut, and found a Best Western where they could lay their heads for the night. Across the street was a chain that served breakfast all day, and they had breakfast for dinner, French toast and bacon for Freddy and an omelet and a sad excuse of a salad for her, iceberg lettuce and a few tomatoes and a thick, sweet dressing. But Susannah didn't mind because eating was a chore. She wanted a cigarette. She wanted wine. She wanted something to steady herself, but instead in her head she kept saying the word *Mom*, like a mantra, *Mom, Mom, Mom*, as in this was what she was doing, this was her purpose. She said to herself, *There are things bigger than you, Susannah. Be grateful for what you have. Be grateful for this boy.*

This was how she kept down the white bear.

After dinner, back in the motel room, Susannah felt something she hadn't felt in a while. She felt that she was of use. It was just the two of them, sharing a room, as they had not done since Freddy was tiny. There were two beds and a TV, the same setup as at any of these places.

It didn't matter to her that Freddy didn't want to be here. It didn't matter that he was acting like a petulant child who had been told he had to go to his grandmother's house when he didn't want to. None of that mattered. All that mattered was that, for the moment, things were suddenly simple again: the two of them against the world, as they were so many years ago when she nursed him on a curb in Queens.

SUSANNAH SURFED CHANNELS ON THE television until she found a movie she thought they both would like, no easy chore. *Close Encounters of the Third Kind* was on, and she remembered it fondly and told Freddy enthusiastically how much he would love it, thinking about Richard Dreyfuss losing his mind and molding all those mashed potatoes into Devils Tower.

But it started slower than she remembered, the kind of movie they don't make anymore, where the build increases the more you invest in it, and it demands your attention. Freddy had no patience. Soon he was curled away from her on his bed, immersed again in his headphones and his music, leaving her to the film that suddenly seemed dated, as did she.

Susannah didn't know who fell asleep first. It was probably her because the last thing she remembered was watching the part where Dreyfuss and the blond woman ride the beat-up old station wagon past the military roadblocks.

But then in the middle of the night, Susannah woke with a start. The television was still on, and Freddy was on his back, breathing deeply with sleep.

Susannah was disoriented at first—the motel, the glow of the television, and the sounds of the highway outside.

It took her a minute to get her bearings. It all came roaring back:

pulling Freddy out of school, emptying the bank account, leaving town as if a wildfire were about to swallow it.

Susannah took a deep breath and looked toward the big plate-glass motel windows that the shades covered but where the pale yellow light of the parking lot and the highway beyond it still seeped in. She had no idea what time it was. It must have been close to dawn by her read of the quality of the light. She imagined everything outside was a fog about to be burned off by the sun. Which was exactly how her mind felt when someone started pounding on the door.

"Susannah," Max's voiced bellowed from the other side. "Open up."

Susannah rose up in the bed. She didn't have time to think. Then Freddy was a blur, out of the bed and past hers and heading toward the door.

"Freddy, no," she said, but it was too late.

Before she could move, he had unlatched the door and Max filled the doorway, the bland early morning light behind him.

"Max," Susannah said.

"Time to go home, Susannah," he said calmly.

"How did you find us?"

"I texted him," Freddy said.

FREDDY TRUSTED MAX. HE THOUGHT maybe it was because every-thing used to seem screwed up before Max. Susannah would have good days and she would have bad days and everything in between. Before Max, Freddy would come home from school and have no idea what was waiting for him. Some days their whole apartment was a shithole, clothes all over the floor, the sink full of dishes, no food in the fridge or the cabinets, and his mom wouldn't get out of bed. Rolling over and with no clothes on, which he didn't need to see, and pointing him to some wadded-up bills on the end table and telling him to go down to the bodega and get whatever he wanted.

But then other days he'd come home and the place would be crazy clean, like so spotless you could eat off the floor and a fridge full of food. Her energy was high and she wouldn't stop talking and she seemed so happy, but it never seemed real, her happiness, a helium kind of happiness that would float away if you let go of the string.

Susannah couldn't handle being alone, Freddy realized. She liked to say to him, "It's just me and you, Freddy," and she said it as if it were the most important thing in the world to say and Freddy wanted to believe her when she said it but he didn't. It felt like one of those things people said when they were out of things to say because everything around them was crappy and uncertain.

When Freddy's dad was alive, Joseph knew how to handle her business, how to take her temperature when she overheated and talk her out of her tree. They say you don't remember things before you are five, but Freddy remembered his dad's voice. His voice stayed with Freddy. His dad's voice was like music, low and steady and always on pitch, the voice of a jazz singer. His words could put you to sleep or they could wake you up, depending on what Joseph wanted to accomplish.

In Freddy's earliest memory, Susannah and Joseph were having an argument. Well, Susannah was yelling at Joseph. And Joseph was talking to her in that voice. Freddy was too young to have any idea what it was about. Freddy drifted out of the bedroom because he didn't like the fighting; it upset him and no one seemed to notice. Freddy went into Joseph's office and turned his swivel chair behind his desk around so that it faced the wall.

Freddy cried. He could hear Susannah shouting, then Joseph's murmur of a voice, her name, "Susannah," he kept saying. Freddy was too young to know anything but that's the thing about kids: just as dogs and bees can sense fear, kids can tell when things are sour and sick.

His dad found him. Freddy felt his dad's hand on his shoulder and his voice in his ear. Freddy didn't turn around, and he didn't lift his head. He was ashamed of his tears.

"Ferdinand," Joseph said in his ear, for he refused to call him Freddy. "It's over now, okay? Your mother, she is better. You can come out."

So Freddy did, and he did over and over, come out after an episode, though he didn't always want to. Then Joseph was gone: a puff of smoke.

THERE HAD BEEN OTHER MEN before Max. Men that Freddy remembered as a bunch of fools, men he came across in the kitchen the morning after, men who scratched their asses and searched for coffee and seemed flummoxed when Freddy walked in and went through the cabinets as if they weren't there, checking the cereal boxes trying to find the ones that still had something in them.

What made Max different, for Freddy, was that he didn't seem like a poser. Freddy could tell that the others who stuck around for more than one night had no interest in him, none whatsoever, but that didn't stop them, he thought, from ladling bullshit on him.

Max, by contrast, never looked down on Freddy. He also didn't blow smoke and sunshine at Freddy. He didn't try too hard. But he also seemed to genuinely care, as if he wanted to know who Freddy was.

And, important, he never tried to be Freddy's dad. That was the big thing. Even after they all moved in together, Max treated Freddy as if he were someone else who lived there, a roommate, a friend. Sometimes Max played the grown-up role, but he didn't overstep it. Kids know if it's fake, and to Freddy there was nothing fake about Max, ever.

FREDDY MADE A MENTAL NOTE of the exit off I-91 in Connecticut and it was all he needed when he stepped into the bathroom—ostensibly to brush his teeth—to text Max and tell him where they were. They could have been anywhere, a sad hotel off a sad highway exit. He texted Max the exit, the hotel, and the room number. He also wrote, *She's acting cray cray, please come.*

Max wrote back instantly. *Hang tight, buddy. On way. Don't say a word. Be there in five hours or less. Go to sleep. Delete this message, k?*

K, Freddy wrote back.

Susannah had some old movie on, something he was supposed to be fired up about, according to her, but it looked ancient, practically black-and-white, with boring old people doing stupid shit and the spaceship that came roaring over the road in the first half didn't even look real. *Learn some special effects, will you?*

He still couldn't sleep, though. Movie or no movie, Freddy was all jacked up. He knew Max was a long way away, but in his mind he worried that Max was going to come barreling through that door any moment and it would all be Freddy's fault. Wasn't this what children feared more than anything else, that it would all be their fault?

Freddy looked over at his mom in the other bed. She hated sleep. He knew this about her. Sleep meant losing control. Susannah was all about control—make the world tiny and you could run it, right? *What you going to do now, Mom? It's just you and me, isn't it?*

Susannah gave him a thin smile. "You like that movie, honey?"

Freddy nodded. "It's cool."

"You sure?" Susannah yawned.

Freddy looked at the small television. A sad-looking family was having dinner and the dad was going batshit all of a sudden, pressing huge amounts of mashed potatoes into a tower on his plate with his hands while everyone watched with horror, which was the part Freddy sort of liked. If it had been cool, it would have been almost funny.

Soon he heard Susannah snoring softly. He reached over and turned off the light between them and he muted the television but kept it on. The only light in the room was the yellowish glow of the television, and Freddy lay there as if Max would be there any minute, picturing him coming through that door, though Freddy knew Max was hours away. Outside Freddy could hear the sound of the highway, the rumble of trucks in the night, and listening to this he fell asleep.

It felt as if moments later Max was there. Freddy bounded out of bed before Susannah had time to know what was happening, opened the door, and gave Max a hug. Freddy saw the look Susannah shot him when he copped to texting Max, but Freddy didn't care. Max would fix it. Max would make it right.

The ride home was a shit show. Max had a rental car, which he left in the parking lot of the motel, stopping long enough to call Avis and tell them where it was, but refusing to do anything beyond just leaving it there with the keys in it. *Badass*, Freddy thought, but he didn't say anything, instead watching as Max, gently, frog-marched Susannah to the front seat of the family Volkswagen, opened the door, put her in there, their bags in the trunk, and climbed in the front, sleepless but looking fresh, and started the engine. The sun was just beginning to rise in the gray dawn.

They rode in silence and Freddy fell asleep once the drone of the tires on the highway began. He slept through Connecticut and much of Massachusetts, but woke when Max stopped at a McDonald's not far from the Vermont border.

Max turned toward the backseat and handed Freddy a twenty. "Run in and get some egg sandwiches and coffee."

Freddy nodded.

"I have to pee," Susannah said.

Freddy sensed it was the first words they had spoken since they left the motel two hours ago. Susannah could be crazy stubborn; she was going to win most blinking contests.

"Okay," Max said. "We all go then."

"Stop treating me like a fucking prisoner."

"Language," Max said.

"Fuck you."

Max waited for Susannah outside the ladies' room while Freddy went and ordered the egg sandwiches and the coffee.

Back in the car, they ate and drank in silence. Freddy put his head-phones back on and leaned his face against the window and watched the land go by, giving way from honky-tonk and suburbia to rolling green hills the closer they got to Vermont.

The coffee jolted Freddy a little bit—he was new to it—but he liked the buzzy feeling it gave him, like the opposite of weed, which he had also recently discovered. He looked up at the two of them in the front seat, the back of their heads, and he smiled a little bit to himself. *It isn't just the two of us, Mom,* thought Freddy. *Not anymore and no matter what you say.*

MAX HAD COME HOME TO an empty house and found evidence everywhere of disarray. Clothes scattered upstairs, toiletries gone from the bathroom, a stray toothbrush on the floor. It was like walking into a crime scene, but a banal one, where the only missing things were clothes and things people cleaned themselves with. In his mind he saw Susannah sweeping their marble bathroom countertop with her hands, filling a plastic bag or something, too urgent to pack carefully.

It occurred to him when he headed up the hill to the university that flight was on her mind, but he thought it far more likely that she would spend the day nervously smoking and seeing boogeymen approaching the door.

He called her: straight to voice mail. He texted, then he texted again. He wrote Freddy. Nothing. He started to panic a little bit.

What if she had gone to the cops? What if she had told them she was in danger, Freddy was in danger, that he had killed David Hammer and she was convinced that Max would kill them, too?

Stop being fucking paranoid, he told himself. That wasn't Susannah's style, and even if it were, nothing evidentiary had changed when it came to David Hammer. Other than that she could tell the police he wasn't born Max W, and that could open a rabbit hole that, if they went down it, would not end well for him. *One thing at a time*, Max told himself. *Don't get ahead of yourself. You just have to find her. In the meantime, stick to facts, goddammit.*

That was when he thought of pulling up his bank account on his phone. They had credit cards, but they generally used the debit, and if Susannah had used it, it might give a clue to where she was. That's when he knew she had fled, really fled, for when he pulled up the app, all the money, every fucking cent of it, was gone. The debit card didn't matter a whit. There was no cash.

Jesus, Susannah.

Max spent that afternoon pacing around the kitchen and ransacking the house like a cop looking for clues to her whereabouts. In her closet, buried under a pile of sweaters, he found a shoebox, and it had some heft to it as he lifted it up and brought it down and carried it over to the bed. He had an odd feeling about opening it, as if he were about to discover a trove of things he wasn't supposed to see, items that belonged to former lovers, gifts she had never returned, letters he shouldn't see, but an image came to him then, far more ominous: a severed head.

Get it together, Max.

But when he opened the box, he just as quickly dropped it with a start. He recoiled from what he saw. The eyes of the fox staring back at him. *What the fuck?* It was on the bed now and he reached down and felt the fur, and it felt prickly and real to his fingers and those marbled eyes looked up at him as if they might blink. Max was not the only one who harbored secrets.

IT WAS A LITTLE AFTER nine when the text from Freddy lit up his phone. Max felt the energy coming back into his body, the optimism that fueled him, and he called a cab and took it out to the small international airport that sat outside the city on a piece of flat land. He wanted to throttle the fat kid in the bad suit behind the counter of the car-rental place who moved as if he were stuck in cement.

"I don't care," said Max. "As long as it runs. Seriously."

Max put it on his credit card, a reminder that that was, for the moment, the only money he had outside of what was in the market and hard to access, credit and debt and not a ton of either. Soon he was out and on the highway and speeding south.

He had plenty of time, he reminded himself. Susannah wasn't going anywhere, not in the middle of the night. He didn't need to go a hundred miles an hour. Max tried to find a radio station to listen to, but the stations kept fading out as he drove through the mountains of Vermont, so eventually he gave up and drove that cheap compact that rattled like tin and listened to the sounds of the tires on the road and the quiet of his racing thoughts.

When he pulled off the highway, it was two a.m. He came into the motel parking lot and circled around the back, and the lot was well lit and there, parked facing the building, was the family Volkswagen. Max pulled in next to it and killed his engine.

He ran his eyes up the building—moving forward in his seat so he could see directly up the windshield—to the door numbers until he saw the one they were in, up on the second floor, their large window, like every motel window at this time of night, blackened and blinded.

Max was suddenly bone tired. It was as if the ride had completely deflated him now that he was here. He had nothing left. The thought of barging in there now and pulling them out and knowing he would have to get right back in the car and drive four hours back the way he had come had almost zero appeal. He pulled out his phone and set the alarm on it for five. He then put the driver's seat back as far as it went and closed his eyes against the light of the streetlamps, and in what felt like seconds, he was fast asleep.

Three hours of sleep helped. Being at the door was a blur, knocking on it, Freddy opening it, Susannah slowly trying to rise in bed but Max seeing in her face her disappointment in herself for not being fast enough, though Max knew she hadn't adequately gamed what she would do because she hadn't anticipated her own son dropping a dime on her. Not that she had a lot of options. She could have called 911 and presented him as the abusive husband. They would have taken her word.

But the door opened and Max smiled.

The jig was up.

By the time they got home—the not talking more exhausting than the talking—Max just wanted to lie down, close his eyes, and rewind the clock four days to the time when they seemed past all of this, and in front of them was the summer, and the first grown-up vacation the three of them had ever taken together.

But that was a luxury he didn't have. He also didn't know where to go from here. His goal was to get them back, and now that that was done, he knew there had to be some reckoning and then a path forward. But that path wasn't clear.

First thing he did when they got into the house and were in the kitchen, Susannah refusing to make eye contact with him, was to slide the shoebox he had found across the counter toward her. "What is this?"

"It's mine."

"I gathered that. But what is it? Open it."

"No." Max saw her glance at Freddy.

"Open it."

She did.

Freddy leaned forward and then back. "What the . . . ?"

"It's a fox. I found it."

"Where?"

"On the street. Nearby."

"And you brought it home?"

"I wanted to keep it. Leave me alone, please. I just want to sleep."

Susannah took the box, covered it, and marched out of the room, heading to the stairs.

"Where's our money?" Max called to her.

"In my bag." Her tone surprised him, suddenly casual, as if he had asked her what time dinner was.

IT ALL FELT OVER TO her. *Drop the curtain now,* Susannah thought, for it was hard to imagine how they came back from any of it. Even if they could, would she even want to? She had been here before, hadn't she?

She left Freddy and Max in the kitchen and went up the stairs. She wanted her phone, but he wouldn't give it to her, not yet. Time was muddled and confused. It was late morning, she thought, though she couldn't be sure of that even. It was sunny outside and warm and the blinds were up in the bedroom and she went to the bed and fell onto it fully clothed and she didn't care about the sun coming in and beaming on her face and she didn't care about anything. She thought that she should cry but she couldn't do that either.

She saw how tired Max was. She had never seen him that tired before. His eyes were blank tiles. She had time. She had time to rest. She needed to rest. She needed to rest before she figured it out. Before she decided what to do next, if she had any moves she could make. Or was it already checkmate?

Joseph was old at the end, not super-old, but Susannah knew he was dying before she knew he was dying, if that makes sense. He had a smell about him in the month or so before, like fruit that had aged past its time in the bowl. She had grown restless and impatient with him: his words, his metronomic voice, no longer slowed her and they no longer soothed her. She didn't want to see his wrinkled face, his sunken eyes, though she never told anyone that. She longed for other men, though that, too, she carried close to her chest, like the fox she had picked up off the road and carried home.

She considered herself a dutiful wife. Her transgressions, such as they were, were limited to brief moments on the street, a handsome man coming up from the subway in his suit adjusting himself on the last step, pushing his hair back and moving into the Manhattan street. Moments that stirred her and suggested that other women lived other lives. That not everyone felt the walls closing in, that the world didn't end when you had a child, that death wasn't yet knocking on the door for everyone's husband.

Max was not Joseph. Despite how tired he looked this morning, he was young, virile, and strong, and they would have had a long life together, right?

The air was close and stale in the room. Susannah got out of bed and went to the window and opened it. She looked out into the back-yard differently from how she ever had, suddenly a prisoner in her own house. A small ledge outside the window ran around the house. It wasn't that high. She imagined climbing out there, then hanging off it to get as close to the ground as she could before letting go. It would hurt, but if she landed right, she'd be just fine. She could run through the backyard and onto the next street. Find a house where someone was home. A woman in distress is a powerful thing. They would let her in. But then what?

She returned to bed. She moved to her side and pressed her face into the pillow. For the next several hours, she slept fitfully, moving in and out of dreams, vague dreams that scared her but that she didn't remember and then woke her up hot in the still room before she fell back half-asleep again.

A few hours later, Susannah gave up. She rolled over on her back and stared at the ceiling. She looked to the window and it was still light out, though she had no idea what time it was. She did not have her phone and she did not wear a watch and it was funny how she felt so unmoored by not having her phone. She listened for sounds but the house was silent.

She rose out of bed, her jeans and her T-shirt crumpled, and she could smell herself, like onions, the need for a shower, the blur the last twenty-four hours had been. She went to the door and out into the hallway. Freddy's door was closed and she passed it, and at the top of the stairs she stopped and listened again, but she heard nothing and she lightly padded down the stairs.

Turning the corner to the living room, she saw Max. He was on the couch, on his back, fast asleep. He was snoring, his head to the side, his mouth slightly agape.

Susannah quickly and quietly moved through the downstairs, looking for Freddy. But Max was the only one downstairs. Freddy had to be in his room, unless he left to go somewhere else.

Susannah made her way back upstairs, stepping on each step carefully, not remembering whether they creaked since she had never had to consider this before.

In the upstairs hallway she made her way to Freddy's door. Normally, she would knock loud enough to overcome headphones or video games and wait for a response before opening the door. It was an acknowledgment of his teenagerhood, the right to privacy that appears as suddenly as puberty.

But today she didn't want to wake Max. She needed Freddy alone for a moment and she needed to explain to him the urgency she felt. This was her failure yesterday: she didn't take the time to explain to him why it was so important they escape. She had treated him like a child. *Give me a do-over*, she wanted to say, *and I know why you texted Max. It's okay, it really is.*

Susannah turned the knob and slowly opened the door. She whispered, "Freddy? It's Mom."

He had his back to her, headphones on, of course. He was at his desk, more of a table, one normally covered with all his junk, whatever he needed for school, skateboard magazines, the small detritus a teenage boy collected in his pockets every day and dumped out like runes.

He was busy, working on something, schoolwork? Some newfound academic interest? Drawing?

She felt disoriented by this, the headphones made sense but the rest of it was foreign.

Susannah walked across the room, still whispering his name, and she didn't want to be loud but she was also worried about startling him.

She put her hand on his shoulder at the same time she screamed, though she didn't remember screaming but she must have, for Max, a few moments later, came flying through the door to see what had happened.

For what Susannah saw when she put her hand on her son's shoulder was what he was doing, the pen poised in his hand, the cardstock note in front of him, finishing the first word in a script she now instantly recognized. All he had written was *you*.

Freddy, for his part, almost jumped out of his skin when he felt her touch. "You can't just come in here."

But they were past that, far past that.

Then Max was there, behind her, he, too, taking it in, a moment for him to absorb it all, to see what she saw, and suddenly, for a second anyway, she and Max were on the same team again. They were parents.

"Why, Freddy?" Susannah said. "Why have you been doing this? Leaving notes for Max? Do you know how much this scared us?"

Freddy shook his head angrily. He wouldn't look at her, only up at Max. "I didn't leave them for you, Max. I left them for her."

IT WAS AS IF ALL the air went out of the room. The middle of the day, the cusp of summer, and the three of them just stood there looking at one another. The air was close and warm. Freddy, who had been tremendously enjoying all the unease, the notes, the secret he'd carried with him for months now, hadn't adequately planned for this moment. He looked from his mom, her motor starting to run, that absent look in her eyes, over to Max, who looked angry. Freddy thought Max might strike him and had never thought that about Max before.

There is memory—the things you remember—and then there is the half-light of memory, the events that for years you can only feel, deep inside you, until they grow and take shape, like stepping away from a mosaic until it comes into stark relief.

That night was like that for Freddy. The older he got, the clearer it appeared to him, the gauzy dream of it giving way to something clearer than sky.

Was it a noise that startled him? Voices in the night?

He was five years old. He was in his narrow wooden bed, the one his parents jokingly called the Pilgrim bed since it was small and wooden and from another time. He woke up from a bad dream and he wanted to cry but instead he lay there with his stuffed bunny tucked close to his body and looked up at the star stickers on the ceiling above his bed. His bedroom faced the alley and the one window always had the blinds pulled down. The alley scared him, how close the other building was with its own windows. He used to worry someone could climb from one of those windows into his own, but his mom said, "Don't be silly, Freddy, no one could do that. It's not possible, honey, okay?"

But the good thing about the alley room was that he couldn't hear any noise from the street. In the other parts of the apartment, sounds drifted up, voices of drunks walking home late at night, sirens, and the horns of the cabbies. But the alley room was like a cocoon. It was usually whisper quiet. It was just Freddy and Bunny and the stars and nothing to bother them, ever.

Lately, his mom and dad had been trying to get him to stay in bed for the night. He often woke, and when he did, he took Bunny and went and climbed in bed with them, sliding his body as close to his mom's as he could.

"You're getting older, Ferdinand," his father said to him. "When you have a bad dream, I want you to take a deep breath, remind yourself it was just a dream, and try to go back to sleep yourself. You can do it."

Freddy gripped Bunny tightly and thought of this while looking up at the stars. But then he heard something, voices coming from the other room, his mom's and dad's. But why were they up?

He climbed out of bed. He walked across his room with Bunny. His door was slightly ajar—he never wanted it completely closed. The apartment was dark except for light coming from his parents' room, from underneath the door, a strip of pale yellow.

He wore red jammies that had padded feet built in, and when he opened his door and stepped out onto the hardwood floor of the narrow hallway, he made no sound as he walked the eight feet that separated his room from his parents'.

At the door, five-year-old Freddy stopped and stood in front of it. He was going to call out, then heard something that sounded like fighting—his mom's voice, followed by his dad's, quieter as usual than his mom's, and this time hers was loud and angry and Freddy didn't like it. He didn't like it at all.

Freddy reached for the handle, turned it, and slowly opened the door. "Mama," he whispered.

But she didn't answer. He opened the door until he was staring at their bed, ten feet away, and he didn't walk in farther for what he saw stopped him and confused him.

His father was on his back, on the side of the bed closest to the door, where he normally slept. His mother, though, was on top of him, straddling him as if she were riding a bike, and she was leaning over his father's head and there was a pillow over his face and she was pressing down on it hard and her face was strained and his father's arms were in the air as if he were doing some kind of weird dance or reaching for her head but he couldn't get there somehow.

She kept pressing harder and harder. His father's hands stopped reaching for her, and his arms fell down like spent balloons. Freddy's mom stopped pressing the pillow down. She let go of the pillow and leaned back like riding a horse into the wind without hands, and she was breathing hard and making a funny sound like crying but not quite.

She was breathing really hard. Harder than she did while running up the three flights of stairs to their apartment, which she did sometimes.

"Mama."

Her head swiveled, took him in. "Freddy. Oh, honey. Go back to bed. I'll be right in."

"I had a bad dream."

"Just go back to your room, honey."

"Can I get in bed with you?"

He watched her run her hands through her hair roughly. "Not tonight, okay, baby? Give Mama a minute and I will be right in."

Freddy covered his face with Bunny and turned around. "Okay, Mama."

He went back to his room. He didn't know why, but he was scared. He lay in the Pilgrim bed and he hugged Bunny tight and he cried and he didn't know why he cried or what he cried for but only that he was confused.

But then his mama was there in his bed with him and she was combing his hair with her fingers and saying, "Hush, baby, hush, it's okay, Freddy," and her arms went around his ribs and pulled him to her boobs and he felt better and fell asleep.

In the morning the apartment was full of men, men in uniforms, other men, and Freddy came out into it all and it was like walking toward the sun. "Mama, what is it?"

He saw she was crying. The tears fell down her face when she talked to the men.

She whispered to the men and came to Freddy. "Come with me." She led him back the way he had come, back into his bedroom, and she got down on her knees in front of him and put her hands on his shoulders and looked him in the eyes but she didn't stop crying.

"Your dad went to heaven."

Freddy pictured her on top of him, pressing and pressing that flat, fat pillow into his face but Freddy didn't say anything. He couldn't say anything. He knew what heaven meant. In time, he would completely forget seeing it, except in that part of him where the past always sang in darkness but could never stay buried forever.

MAX FELT THE WEIGHT IN the room. The room was fucking pregnant with the weight of everything. Max looked at Freddy, still sitting down, that one word written, *YOU,* so perfect, and part of Max wanted to make Freddy finish the note right here and right now. *Tell us what you can't actually tell us, you little bitch.*

"Freddy," Max said sternly. "Look at me, Freddy. Why are you writing these notes? Did you write all of them? The three on the door?"

Freddy nodded.

Max stepped back and felt how coiled he was, his muscles in his legs tight as if he were about to jump, and the vein in his neck that popped when he was stressed. He looked over at Susannah. She looked as if she was about to crack, the panic coming, wolves clawing at the door, but he was so far beyond giving a fuck. He thought of David Hammer, going under and rising up, the surprise on his face, Max's hands on his shoulders, and then the rock as Max slammed into it and sank in the turbulent spring water.

"Why?" Max asked. "Why did you write them?"

Freddy looked away. He looked toward the wall. He wouldn't look at either of them.

"Tell me, Freddy," Max said, raising his voice just a hair.

Freddy turned back and met Max's eyes, though he still wouldn't acknowledge his mother. Freddy's eyes were damp with tears being held back.

"She killed my dad."

"Freddy? What?" Susannah said. "Why are you saying this?"

"I watched you. You didn't think I would remember. But I did. I was there. I saw you. I saw all of it. You on top of him. Suffocating him."

"Honey, no. Really. This is crazy."

"You're crazy," Freddy spat back.

They were silent then, the two of them, staring at each other, and Max looked from Freddy to Susannah. Freddy looked resolute and relieved, and Susannah looked tight, her face that brittle mask that came on in moments of great panic. Looking at the two of them, Max knew that Freddy had spoken the truth. That Susannah had killed Joseph and that Freddy had witnessed it. Max could feel that truth in his bones the way you can feel the cold of winter when it first arrives.

Max looked at his wife and he saw her differently all of a sudden. He saw her as he first saw her, back when she took his breath away as he came off the elevator expecting someone else entirely, that crazy rawboned beauty she had, the red hair and the deep brown eyes, as if the years were stripping away in front of him. It was funny how this happened sometimes: the way people we know will build layers over time, practically dermal, so that it takes something like this to see them again as we once did, when they were new and pure, a blank canvas waiting for lust to be painted on it.

THE FEAR, FOR SUSANNAH, ALWAYS came back to feeling trapped. Small spaces, tall buildings, elevators, airplanes, subways, traffic, even lines in the supermarket. All around her, her entire life, makeshift prisons had emerged, some of her own creation, others handed to her by others and from which she had to break out.

For it was when the walls closed that the white bear came.

Susannah wasn't a horse to be broken. But sometimes that's what it felt that Joseph was up to: he was trying to break her with his games. Come to think of it, her father was the same way, though he did not play games. He practiced beliefs, things he carried deep about how to live, though when you got right down to it, she wasn't sure there was any difference, at least in the end result. It was always about control, it was always about putting her in a box and saying, *You are stuck here.*

Other couples lied and didn't show the world all their truths, but the ones that she and Joseph hid were different, were they not? No one could know he still treated her. That she was his client, his patient.

This wasn't a secret so much as it was an agreed-upon lie. Every couple had an origin story—*Hey, how did you guys meet?* And they didn't shy away from theirs. They told different variations, but this was to be expected. "He was my therapist," Susannah might say, or "One day she showed up in my office," said Joseph. "It was love at first sight," and on and on and on.

But they never told the real story and they couldn't tell the real story for Joseph could lose his license. He should have stopped treating her the moment they slept together, not that even that would have passed an ethical smell test, but it would at least have shown a willingness to acknowledge a lapse and to do things differently.

Instead, they had been together six years and he was still bringing her in once a week, to that chair across from him, the ticking clock on the shelf behind, the painting of the mountain and the valley above it, vaguely Buddhist and poorly done. Such a cliché of what a progressive therapist in New York would hang on the wall. *Stare at this blandness, people,* it said, *and know that I am righteous and kind.*

Joseph believed he was the only who could cure her. He thought he alone held the key that could unlock her mind. But honeymoons are honeymoons for a reason, and after a time, she had lost faith in what he could do for her, that maybe it was time for her to not be in treatment. Therapy could be a trap like any other. Sometimes it ran its course, as she knew Joseph told other patients, but he had never said that to her. Instead, it was a weekly expectation, like church when she was a kid.

A night in December: outside the windows of their apartment snow fell in the city and Susannah liked snow in the city at night, how it muffled the sounds of the traffic, how, for a moment, everything looked clean and brand-new. Tonight, though, she didn't care.

Joseph had put Freddy to bed because she couldn't. She was too upset—she and Joseph had had their weekly session, and afterward, when they ate a dinner of Chinese takeout, Joseph reminded her that she needed to keep that wall intact, the one between a session and the rest of their life.

The rage came over her like a winter wind, but not in front of Freddy, she wasn't going to do that, which was another way of pushing the bear down when she shouldn't. Instead she seethed silently, but Joseph knew, and Freddy probably knew, too, because kids felt energy the way dogs do.

In session that day, Joseph had made her close her eyes for he was always making her close her eyes. In the years she had been seeing him, her husband, her therapist, whatever followed closing her eyes was sure to be something that unsettled her.

Susannah had been jittery all day, before the session and even more so once it started, one of those days when the panic seemed about to breach the walls she had put up and come rushing in like a dam-burst of water. She didn't want to play games, not today. She told Joseph this, too, letting him know that on a scale of one to ten, her baseline today was about a four, and so please could they just talk today? Maybe they could talk about pleasant things? Maybe they could talk about the future, about dreams, about possibilities to lift both of them out of this moment, this small room with the snow tumbling outside the window?

But Joseph had different ideas and he ignored her.

"Close your eyes, Susannah," he said in his measured, calm voice.

"No, not today. I won't."

"Close your eyes."

"Can we just talk?"

"Close your eyes, Susannah."

She did.

"The door closes," he said. "The elevator begins to move. A moment later it rocks hard, lurches, comes to a stop. The lights go out. It is just you—"

"No." Susannah opened her eyes. "I won't. Not today."

Joseph leveled his dark eyes at her. "Get in the crate," he said coldly.

"No, Joseph."

"Get in the crate." He looked at her as if he were going to stare right through her. His eyes were hypnotic, commanding.

Susannah looked over to the corner of the room where Joseph kept a dog crate, though they didn't have a dog. He'd bought it for this purpose, though she knew he told patients that he had a Labrador that some days he brought to the office. He had gotten the crate for her, and they had only tried it once and she swore never again.

But she rose out of her chair as if in a dream and went to it, opened it, and got down on all fours and climbed in. Joseph had gotten out of his chair when she had gotten out of hers, and behind her he closed the door to the crate and latched it shut. It was only large enough for her to fit on all fours or curled awkwardly. Joseph put a blanket over it and it was dark and she began to cry. She heard his footfalls across the room, and then the door to his office opening and closing. He left her in there, barely able to move, her back up against cold narrow bars, and for an hour she cried and she screamed and no one heard her.

In her head, among the competing voices, was her own steady one, her best-self voice. *Never again*, she told herself. *Never again*.

When he released her, Susannah pushed past him and went right down the stairs and out into the street.

She wasn't wearing a coat and the snow that fell was heavy and sticky, clinging to the trees and the stop signs. She let it fall on her and she breathed in the cool winter air and she listened to the sounds of the cars on the wet pavement in front of her, but she didn't see any of it because of the profound ringing in her head and she knew she needed out. If it were not for Freddy, she would just run now, up the avenue, and run until she reached the park and could disappear inside it.

That night, Susannah pretended to sleep while Joseph read next to her. She could hear his breathing as he read, the occasional clearing of his throat, the clogged sinuses he refused to blow, all the things she had grown to hate. When he fell asleep, she rose up and gently removed his reading glasses, placed them on the end table, took his book from his clasped hands, and put that on the end table, too.

She was determined to be patient. She listened to him snore, the apnea he had never treated, those moments when his body shuddered and went still. She listened to the deep snores that cascaded down and then came quickly to an end, the dead stop, his dying for a second.

Then she rolled over and climbed on top of him, and at the moment the snore stopped, she snuffed him out like a candle. His arms reached up toward her face. He then went dark. It was so easy.

Never again, she told herself. She was so focused that she never saw her Freddy standing there, watching.

THEY LEFT FREDDY IN HIS room. It was only midafternoon, but the day had been like five days, each one its own segment, starting with an awkward dawn at a Connecticut motel on the side of the highway. Max was out of his mind. All he could muster before they left Freddy was that they would talk about it later, and that was mostly because his focus had shifted so suddenly, with the power this woman had over him when she tripped into good lighting, as she had the moment he realized she had killed Joseph.

Everything else was now secondary to his lust. Relief would come later—when it would sink in that no one was, in fact, aware of his past. No colleagues were out there waiting in the wings and trolling him with handwritten notes. The whole thing was fucking Freddy.

In their bedroom, they practically crashed together—the door barely closing behind them and then locked, before Max pushed Susannah against the wall and she said, "Oh, really," and he responded, "Yes, that's right."

Susannah moved against the wall, and Max said, "Get your hands up," as if he were arresting her, and she did, put her hands with her palms flat on the wall above her head.

Oh, how he loved the curve of her from here, the way her back sloped down to her waist, the rise of her full ass under her jeans, those hips that he put his hands on as he leaned forward and kissed the back of her neck as if he meant it. It was primal, urgent sex this time, her pants coming down until she stepped out of them, his dropping to just past his knees, his hand wrapping around and silencing her mouth as he drove into her.

Afterward, they fell apart and they stood breathing hard and staring at each other like adversaries. Max looking deep into her brown eyes and Susannah looking deep into his and he broke it first by laughing. He started to laugh and she did, too, her hands on her hips, her whole body convulsing with laughter.

They went to the bed and they both fell back on it, side by side and onto their backs, not looking, like some corporate trust exercise. Susannah rolled into the crook of his arm. Max put his arm around her shoulder and she cuddled into him.

For a moment they didn't talk. They were still breathing hard.

Susannah said, "I killed him."

"I know."

"How did you know?"

"I believed Freddy. I could just tell. He didn't make it up. And it wasn't some kind of repressed-memory thing where he imagined it and you couldn't tell what was real."

"Yes," Susannah said softly. "I can't believe he has carried this with him."

"Why did you do it?"

"Kill Joseph?"

"Yes."

"He was cruel."

"Oh, you never said."

"There was no point. He was dead. Don't you think children should be able to mythologize their fathers?"

"I don't know. I didn't know mine. Only saw him once."

"Freddy never knew. He was too young."

"Tell him. Tell him about the cruelty. Freddy just wants to know the truth about things. He will believe you."

Susannah looked up at the ceiling. She looked at the fan, which wasn't moving and which she never liked anyway—she never understood ceiling fans. They looked silly and didn't do much.

She nodded, more to herself. "Okay. I will."

THAT NIGHT SHE AND FREDDY walked together out of the neighborhood and over to the university, where they sat under a big oak tree and looked down the hill to the city below them and the lake beyond it. Susannah made him look at her and she told him she loved him, loved him more than anything, and for that reason she had never told him the truth about his father. But Freddy was old enough now and didn't deserve to be gaslighted about it, not anymore.

She talked for a while. It felt good to talk, an unburdening she didn't know she needed until she was doing it. These stories she had never told anyone in their entirety, not even Rose.

She told her son that, when she met Joseph, she was in crisis and he knew how to calm her down. He was her doctor. For that reason, she fell in love with him but soon that love turned into a prison.

"He had a big gifted mind, your father. But he was not a good man. He trapped me. He played with my head until I didn't know who I was anymore. He wouldn't let me breathe."

"Why didn't you just leave?"

Susannah sighed. "I asked myself that same thing for years. But he had brainwashed me into thinking I couldn't. That there was nowhere I could go, and that no one would believe me if I told them why I left. Who was going to believe me, an art-school dropout? When you had the Harvard Ph.D. telling you what was really happening? And I was the one with the history of mental illness."

"So you killed him?"

Susannah sighed. She took her time with this one. The night was warm and even though they were in the middle of the city, there was no moon and the stars arced away from the two of them and over the lake.

"Technically yes."

"Technically?"

"I helped him die. Have you heard of assisted suicide? Where people are sick and they want to die to end the pain?"

"Is that what he wanted?"

"He was sick, Freddy. His heart wasn't good. He wasn't healthy. Yes, I put a pillow over his mouth, but only for a minute. A healthy man would have been fine. I'm sorry. I'm sorry I did it and I'm sorry most of all you had to see it."

Susannah started to cry and the tears that came were real, she hadn't planned on this part, and something about it was so genuine that she saw Freddy's look change, his own big brown eyes, the eyes of her father, not her eyes and not Freddy's father's, eyes that skipped a generation, of her father that never knew him and only saw him once, a lifetime ago on a doorstep in Queens. This made her cry more, and suddenly it was Freddy who was consoling her.

"Mama." It had been a long time since he had called her this. He put his arms out for her and she said, "Oh, my baby, my baby boy," and he said, "Don't call me that," but she did anyway and she brought him close to her.

Around them people walked by in the dark. The stars were overhead. To their left, cars went down the slope of Main Street to the restaurants and the clubs. And none of it mattered.

THEN NORMALCY DESCENDED AS EASILY as after a thunderstorm. It was as if the weather just needed to break, shake off the humidity, and suddenly it was glorious, beautiful summer.

Freddy finished out the school year, Susannah felt a clarity she didn't know she was capable of, and on a hot Thursday afternoon in June, Max took a plane to New York City to open for Bon Jovi and speak to his largest room ever, and one full of bankers.

He felt strong. Coming over the Queensboro Bridge in the town car they had waiting for him, he could look down and see the neighborhood where Susannah had grown up—but his focus was not there, it was on the big city in front of him, the buildings rising like castles across the river.

This is how to travel, Max thought. *Get off the plane and a chauffeur is waiting with a sign that says MAX W. He takes your bag and you sink into the soft leather seats in the back of a large car.*

The driver took him to the Ritz-Carlton on Central Park South. It was a lovely day in the city, not too hot for the time of year, and a little after eleven-thirty in the morning Max climbed out of the cab. His talk was at three. The driver said he would pick Max up at two-fifteen for the ride down to West Street and the Goldman Sachs offices.

They had gotten Max a suite on the eighteenth floor, big windows with views of all Central Park.

"Holy shit," Max said to himself after the bellhop had closed the door and left him alone. He wanted to bring Susannah but she was sensitive to the mending of things with Freddy. Max wanted to say that perhaps the best way to mend with Freddy was to go away. Space is a healer. But he left her alone. That said, the room was astonishing—a separate large living room, three televisions, a sitting area for eight or so, and a bedroom with a king bed, a huge bathroom covered in marble. This was how the rich traveled—or artists if Goldman was paying.

Max went to the window. He had never seen the park from this height before. The trees from above looked as if they were painted, golden green, and the people and the horse-drawn carriages moving on the pathways looked like toys. Max had slept in the park many times back in the day—often up in trees, which made it easier to avoid detection. It was a practiced art, sleeping in trees, knowing how to stay still, to not roll over, for to roll over meant you would fall and get badly hurt. Some nights it would storm in the middle of the night and the rain would fall in sheets and he would wake to it, soaking him, making the branches of whatever tree he had found to suit his body slick with it. He had never thought much about the buildings that framed the park. They might as well have been on another planet. They were heights that could not be scaled. Now here he was, at the top.

He ordered a room-service lunch. A steak frites, hold the frites, Cobb salad, a bottle of Châteauneuf-du-Pape, and a bottle of Pellegrino.

It was good to be Max. He ate voraciously. The wine tasted like raisins. He paced around the hotel room and stared down at Columbus Circle and the city that stretched north toward the Bronx.

At quarter to two, he showered and dressed in his standard

outfit, the white T-shirt, the jeans, the black sneakers. The car waited for him when he emerged out of the hotel, and Max smirked a little bit when the doorman holding the car door open for him to slide in the back said, "Have a good afternoon, Mr. W."

The car drove down Fifth Avenue in the midafternoon crawl of traffic. The streets slammed with people, many with oversize shopping bags. The cavalcade of commerce was all around him, commerce that artists normally stood in some measure in opposition to. But not Max, at least not secretly: for life was leading him to the most hallowed halls of capitalism, where they were going to pay him fifty thousand dollars to tell a bunch of suits how to be better versions of themselves.

But then again, Max thought, looking out the window at the throngs he, as a gutter punk, used to mock, who better to do that? If it was the American dream they were selling, who embodied that more than he did?

At the Goldman Sachs building, Max was brought up to the third floor and then to a back room, which was to be his greenroom. They had water and snacks and other things for him.

The woman responsible for him was otherworldly beautiful, mixed race with a wild thatch of hair and caramel eyes.

"Anything you need?" she asked.

Max shook his head. "I have everything."

And he did. He had everything.

Ten minutes later, he walked into a giant room, full of desks everywhere, but also full of people standing, thousands and thousands of men and women all dressed to the nines in beautiful suits. There was a small stage, a single microphone. Max climbed onto the stage and they began to clap, and they clapped more, and soon all he could hear was the steady and unceasing drone of their applause. He smiled big and wide and walked to the center of the stage and took the microphone off its stand.

Max looked out into the crowd and let the applause go. They were so pretty, all those people filling this magnificent room. Masters of the universe, thought Max. So fucking pretty, the lot of them. On top of the world they were, and now he was, too.

He permitted himself a long, long pregnant pause.

"Be the art. For you are the art." He dropped the microphone to his side for a second and just smiled and took in the room. He had them already.

WHILE MAX WAS IN NEW YORK, Susannah dropped Freddy off at the skate park down at the edge of the lake and next to the railroad tracks. The beautiful day was sunny and mild, with a warm wind coming off the lake. She sat in the car for a moment and watched him, so independent this boy of hers, the board under his arm as he walked away from her. A group of similar-age kids were swooping around the wooden bowl, doing tricks off the edges. She watched Freddy reach them and put his board down on the edge, balance his feet, and she held her breath as he zoomed down toward the bottom, his arms out from his sides like wings. He was out of her view for a second before rising up again on the side, turning skillfully and shooting back down again.

You can't keep him in a bubble, Susannah, she told herself.

She drove to the big cooperative market in the middle of town. They were low on fruit and bread and milk and she had this idea of cooking something elaborate, even though it was only going to be Freddy and her for dinner. She had not eaten much other than her morning smoothie and it was always a bad idea to go food shopping when hungry. She went over ideas in her head and settled on roasting a rack of lamb if they had it. In her mind it was more winter food, but she was imagining smearing it with mustard and rolling it in bread crumbs and then slicing it through the bones, perfectly medium rare, and the two of them indelicately picking up those lollipops of meat and nibbling on the gamy pieces closest to the bone. She would rub the roast with rosemary and garlic, too, and scatter more rosemary sprigs around the pan so that the whole kitchen filled with the rich smell of them. Max was certainly eating at some three-star restaurant on his night there. Maybe that was why she wanted to cook something fancy. Was she being competitive?

Susannah didn't like grocery stores. She much preferred the open farmers' market. She hated lines, and while this co-op could get busy, if she hit it at the right time, she could often make it through quickly. The middle of the afternoon, as it was now, or midmorning during the school year, were the only times she would generally go. If she went at lunch, it was crowded with people getting sandwiches, and forget about coming in at five o'clock when everyone got off work and was rushing through to buy food for dinner.

Coming in the door, Susannah got a cart and came into the produce section and began to move up and down the small aisles, looking for what was good, shopping like an old Spanish woman, shopping like her mother. The asparagus were tempting but looked past their prime, but then she saw the smallest broccoli florets, from a local farm, and they were the brightest of greens and looked as if they had just been plucked from the soil.

She was filling a plastic bag with these when she felt a hand on her shoulder and a woman's voice saying into her ear in Spanish, "I know you have a story to tell."

Susannah turned quickly and there was the detective, Susannah couldn't remember her name—Scott? Wilson? something like that, something bland and white sounding—and Susannah almost didn't recognize her in street clothes, tight-fitting jeans and a T-shirt, her hair down, shiny and curly to her shoulders. Susannah had not before thought of her as pretty, or as having a life outside of the uniform, but now suddenly it dawned on Susannah that the woman probably had an entire life outside of her work, maybe children at home and a husband, or perhaps a wife. This was Vermont. And she was pretty, surprisingly so. Her skin smooth and nut brown, a slightly lighter shade than her eyes.

Susannah didn't like this intrusion. Max said it was over. She looked at the woman. "I don't tell stories, Detective."

"Dolores. That's my name when I'm not working."

"You act like you're working."

"I'm shopping."

"Well, me, too . . . Excuse me." Susannah pushed her cart past Dolores.

"Susannah. Wait."

Susannah stopped.

"Let me buy you a coffee."

Susannah imagined this, the two of them sitting together, holding cups of lattes in both hands in front of their faces, looking at each other. This came with a pang of remembrance, of New York and of Rose, of what it meant to have women friends you could talk to.

Susannah surprised herself by saying, "Okay."

Dolores smiled. "Great."

They found an uncrowded aisle in which to park their carts, pushing them against a row of paper towels. In the front of the store, set off from the rest, was a small café—a barista counter and a smattering of wooden tables. Dolores bought two iced lattes and they found a two-top next to the window and sat down.

Dolores had an intelligent face, Susannah thought—something about her eyes, large and chocolate brown, almost without white. They looked both kind and knowing.

"How do you like Vermont?" Dolores asked.

"It's been great. I mean, other than what happened. That was a nightmare."

"Do you miss New York?"

"Some things about it. But mostly no. It's good for Freddy here. I used to worry so much about him. Do you have kids?"

"Not yet. I'm not sure I want them. I keep thinking something is wrong with me for thinking that."

"Well, I don't want any more," said Susannah with a small laugh. "One was enough for me. But it is a beautiful thing. Especially when they are little. Now, it's different."

"Freddy is from your first marriage?"

"Yes."

"Where is his dad? In New York?"

"No, he died ten years ago. He was older. A psychologist."

"Ah. I thought I would be a psychologist. It was my major at the university."

"I didn't know you went to the university."

Dolores laughed. "Don't act so surprised. Yeah, came here from the Bronx. That first year was really hard. I was so homesick. And so cold."

"But you stayed."

"It got easier. And I fell in love with Vermont. I hate traffic. It's easy here."

"It must be weird being a cop."

"My father was a cop. NYPD. I never thought I would be. We all become our fathers or our mothers, don't you think? Girls usually their mothers. I went the other way, I guess."

Susannah considered this. She saw her mother, small and mousy, old-fashioned, her house a hearth to silently tend to. Susannah pictured her gruff, strict father, leaving every morning for work, how proud he was. Was she either of them? She didn't think so.

"Are you married?"

"Not yet. And yes, I'm straight. If you were wondering. People always wonder about female cops. Just haven't met the right one yet. Vermont is a hard place to date, you know?"

"I bet."

"Where did you meet Max?"

Susannah told her the story instinctively, the way she had always told it, though as soon as she said he had crashed the party pretending to be someone else, she regretted it, innocent though it was, but with everything she knew now she worried she was allowing this woman, this cop, a window into her husband that could be dangerous.

"He swept you off your feet then."

"Pretty much." Susannah nodded.

"It's a beautiful story, every girl's dream. See? I told you: you did have a story to tell."

Susannah looked at her phone, at the time. "I should go. Thanks for the coffee."

"By the way, how is Max holding up? You know, with all this. He seemed pretty broken up."

"He's okay. I think he will live with it forever. Like anyone would."

"Just imagine how Joanie Hammer must feel. Her love just taken away from her like that."

Susannah was aware of Dolores's eyes on her and she met them. She saw them searching her face and she determined not to give her anything. She needed to be outside.

"Thanks again for the coffee." Susannah stood up.

"Of course. And, Susannah, here's my card." Dolores slid it across the table to her. "I know I gave it to you before. But call me anytime, okay? I enjoyed this."

Susannah nodded. She turned and walked away. She went to the door, the sliding doors, and through them and out into the parking lot and the summer day. She left her cart in the aisle and she knew Dolores would notice this but Susannah didn't care. She needed to fly.

When Susannah went to pick Freddy up at the skate park, he was with his friend Ivan, a skinny blond kid.

"Ivan wants to know if I can sleep over," Freddy said.

Susannah looked at Ivan, his shorts cut-off cords below the knees, his T-shirt with a picture of Bob Marley holding a joint in his fingers. Ivan reminded her of boys she knew in high school and Susannah wondered if the shirt was just an affect or if the boys were already smoking pot. She had never smelled it, but kids were clever these days. She was about to say that tonight wasn't a good night, that Freddy and she had plans, but she saw the pleading in Freddy's eyes, and she knew Ivan's parents both worked at the university, too, and this gave her some comfort, even though she didn't know them. Ivan's father taught biology or something and his mom was at the hospital.

"Okay." She nodded.

"Can you give us a ride there?" Freddy asked.

"Get in."

Ivan's parents lived in the south end of town, a web of narrow streets and close-together small houses, and Susannah went to the door with them and Ivan's mother was home, a tall slender woman wearing overalls. They talked on the porch for a moment, and Susannah felt better about Freddy's staying over.

"You know they're just going to lock themselves upstairs and play video games," Ivan's mother said.

Susannah laughed. "They would do the same at my place."

Back at home, Susannah was suddenly aware of the emptiness of the house. She wanted to be one of those people who loved being alone, but she was not. In the kitchen she heard the steady tick of the clock and she turned and looked at it: it was a few minutes past four. She went to the refrigerator and found a half-drunk bottle of chardonnay and pulled it out, slipped the cork out, and poured herself a full glass.

She walked around the house with her wine, through the kitchen, into the wide hallway that led to the front living room, its white walls and bright light from the tall windows. She wondered what Max was doing right now, if he was done with his talk yet. She pictured him in the city, probably at some hotel bar, sipping a vodka tonic, the adrenaline coming off him in waves. That adrenaline he had after being onstage, when she knew he was all sex, an animal masculinity that could fill a room. An old tinge of jealousy came over her, and it was irrational but she couldn't help it. Max had never strayed. It wasn't his thing. But part of her was bothered he hadn't suggested she join him.

She drank her wine. It occurred to her, almost as an afterthought, that she hadn't eaten since breakfast. The wine was going to her head. She took out her phone and dialed Max. It went right to voice mail.

"Hey, it's me. I hope it went well. Okay, bye."

She drank her wine and waited for the call back. One glass turned into two, and the clock, when she went back into the kitchen, said it was past five.

Susannah opened the fridge and peered into it. She moved some things around, pondering dinner. *You should just go out,* she told herself. *Like you used to sometimes, like you did in New York.*

She put the empty glass of wine in the sink and went upstairs. She stripped off her clothes, dropped them on the floor, and took a hot shower. She blew her hair out and put on mascara and a subtle lipstick. In her closet she found a small black dress, slipped it over her head, went to the mirror, and surprised herself by how well it still fit, that it still hung in the right way and in the right places. Black heels completed the look, and when she was done, she admired herself in the mirror and maybe it was the wine but she liked what she saw looking back.

"I'd fuck me," she said out loud, then laughed.

Susannah drove downtown. She parked in the garage on Cherry Street, then walked out and onto the street. In front of her was the lake, shimmering and blue in the early sunny evening. It had been a long time since she had done anything like this. She felt electric.

She went into the lobby of the swanky new Hotel Vermont, which had gone up in the last year. The people who worked there all wore flannel shirts and jeans, some touristy idea of Vermont, and she made her way through the lobby to the bar.

The bar was half full, and at tables behind it people were having dinner. The doors were open to the outside, and through them she could see a slice of lake. She made her way down the copper-topped bar and took a seat with room on either side of her.

"Something to drink?" asked the handsome young bartender, also in flannel, despite the warmth.

"A martini, dirty as you can make it. And a burger. Fries."

"Preference on gin?"

"You choose."

"How do you like your burger?"

"Medium rare."

The drink came. Susannah looked down the bar, young couples mostly, and she was waiting for her food when her phone started to buzz. It was Max. She looked down at it, the vibrating pulse of it like something trying to lure her out of a dream. She ignored it, saw the voice-mail message light up, and ignored that, too.

The food arrived and Susannah knew she needed to eat, but something happened to her sometimes when she drank. She just wanted more of the martini and didn't want to eat, which was a terrible idea. She picked at the fries and forced herself to take a few bites of the burger.

A text from Max lit up her phone. *Where are u?*

Susannah ordered another drink. A few seats down the bar sat a pretty couple, and after a few minutes of eavesdropping she realized they were on a first date. They had met for a drink and it was going well. They were now ordering food. Susannah watched the woman lean forward as he spoke, all her body language saying, *You can have me.* Susannah remembered that feeling, what it was like to be new with someone, the electric excitement of the unknown. She remembered how in those moments you don't know each other at all, and that is part of it, too. An undertone of fear comes from two people each giving themselves up, becoming vulnerable.

Susannah thought of Dolores Scott today, sitting at the table at the co-op, handing her the business card and saying, "Imagine what Joanie feels."

So maybe fear didn't only reside in new love. Could you ever really know someone?

"Anyone sitting here?" a voice next to Susannah said, bringing her back to the moment. She looked up to see a man a little older than her, a handsome head of hair and a dark beard, white button-down shirt, crisp jeans, and an expensive watch.

"All yours," she said.

"Thanks."

Susannah looked straight ahead as he slid in next to her. She sipped her martini. She could smell him, the man next to her, deodorant maybe, not cologne, but pleasant, like leather. The bartender arrived and the man ordered a rye old-fashioned, and Susannah pushed her half-eaten meal toward the bartender, who swept it up wordlessly and with one hand.

Susannah leaned back on her barstool, allowing the man next to her to see her, the curve of her under her dress. She liked being watched. She didn't even have to look at him to know his eyes were on her. She came forward again, reached for her martini glass, and snuck a glance at him from the side of her eye.

"Do you live here?"

She looked up at him, as if surprised. "Yes, I do."

"It's a beautiful town. The lake is magnificent."

"And you?"

"I'm just here for meetings. I live in New York. First time here. Quick flight. I should come more often."

His old-fashioned arrived, the bartender placing it in front of him.

"I used to live in New York," Susannah said. "West Village."

"I'm downtown. Tribeca."

"What do you do?"

"I work in tech. How about you?"

"I'm an artist," Susannah found herself saying, though it had been a long time since she had thought of herself that way.

"Do you paint? Teach?"

"Both. I paint. And I teach at the university." She surprised herself with how easily this lie rolled off her tongue, what it felt like to pretend to be someone else, if only for a moment.

"Well, I'm impressed. I'm Michael."

"Susannah."

They talked, and as they did, Susannah found herself creating a whole new her. She wasn't a housewife, she wasn't a mom; she had never had a child, wasn't for her, you know? Instead the commitment to her practice was so complete, she had hardly had time for men, other than for those important needs, if he knew what she meant. (He nodded and smiled, as if to say he did.) The portrait she drew for him was of a powerful woman who had made her way through the scrappy art world of New York, had traveled much, risen up through academia, all while leaving a trail of broken hearts behind her.

"Well, let me ask you something then," he said, finally stopping her in a way that made her realize she had been talking for a while, a mania she didn't know she needed to exorcise.

"Sure." She nodded.

"Then what's with the wedding band?"

Susannah looked down and she laughed. "I wear it to keep men like you from hitting on me."

He smiled. "Oh, is that what I'm doing?"

"You know what you're doing." She touched his knee as she said it.

This was what she wanted, all she wanted, that moment when she could feel the desire radiating off him, to know that she could summon it, that this man who had forty minutes before never seen her was now imagining her without her clothes, his hands moving over her, what it would be like to be inside her.

By the time they left the bar together, Susannah realized she was drunk. The bar had filled up since she arrived, and he led her through the crowd that had gathered at the other end, and past the band setting up to play in the lobby, three long-haired young guys unpacking amplifiers and microphone stands.

"Come upstairs with me," he whispered in her ear as they walked.

She shook her head and laughed. "You wish."

As they came around the lobby toward the elevators, she felt his hand on her back guiding her toward them. As they entered the empty foyer that housed the elevators, Susannah spun him around quickly, so that he was against the wall. She moved against him and he went for her mouth with his lips, but she moved her head away from him, and his lips fell on the side of her neck. She pushed into him and she felt his hands sliding down her back and he was pulling her tight. Susannah kicked her head back, felt his mouth hot on her neck. Then she pushed him in the chest, hard, and he said, "Hey," but she didn't care.

She stepped away from him. She was quite drunk. She looked at his face. He was good-looking, so symmetrical, all those lines, a perfect nose, his even-shaped blue eyes, the line of his dark beard, sculpted. She laughed.

"Why are you laughing?"

Susannah laughed more. It was cartoonish laughing but she couldn't help it. She twirled her finger toward his face, small circles, and turned around. She sashayed away from him, aware of his eyes on her ass.

"Wait. What the fuck?"

But she didn't stop. She moved back out into the lobby and she didn't look back. She went past the front desk and then out the front doors to the street. There was no way she should be driving but she was going to make it home.

THE RIDE HOME WAS NOT long but, to Susannah, it might as well have been a safari. She gripped the wheel tightly with both hands and focused on keeping it straight, on stopping fully at the lights, on getting the car up the hill, which was what she repeated to herself: *Up the hill and a right turn and you are safe. Just don't fucking hit anything, please.*

By some miracle, she made it onto her street, then down it, and pulled in the driveway. Not until the following morning would she see that she'd left the car parked on a hard diagonal, the only evidence of the danger she had narrowly avoided.

She barreled into the house, her legs suddenly unsteady, forward momentum taking her into the kitchen. She thought for a moment about smoking a cigarette, then felt the gin rising in her throat and just made it in time to the sink, where she emptied herself.

Susannah stood for a while after, the sink against her back, in case more was to come. She took out her phone and had fifteen texts from Max, increasingly frantic, but she couldn't get herself to do anything. All she needed was to take a moment and write him back and say something like *I'm so sorry, I lost my phone.* Or *My phone died.*

But she couldn't do even that. Her head spun. She was numb and felt terrible.

She stumbled upstairs. She managed to brush her teeth, slide the dress off and onto the floor. She went to the bed and let the sleep come, not elusive this night, though she knew the morning would bring other problems.

AFTER MAX LEFT GOLDMAN, HE was on such a high he eschewed the car they had waiting to whisk him back to the hotel. He wanted to walk. He wanted to be on the streets again, this old New York, the anonymity of it all, just another guy walking down the cobblestones of lower Manhattan. The day was pleasant and warm and even in the midafternoon the streets were full. The smells of the city were everywhere, cigarette smoke and garbage piled around streetlamps, truck exhaust, and the sounds, too, the beeping of horns, the grinding of brakes, the cacophony of voices as he passed people, different languages coming to him as music rather than as words.

Fifty fucking thousand dollars and for what? Not that Goldman cared, since they probably paid Bon Jovi a cool million. Max had passed the band on his way out, the aging hair rockers, Jon Bon giving him a "Hey, man" as Max walked by them.

Max had killed, though. They were better than a college audience. They were amped from the moment he got onstage. It was less about him and more about their energy. Audiences had their own ecosystems and sometimes it was simply a matter of holding up a mirror and reflecting their energy back. The great speakers all did this, harnessed that power that didn't come from them but from the mass of the people in front of them. One of these days, Max thought, maybe he would teach people how to do this. Maybe he would tell them that the amazing thing about addressing a crowd was that they are never thinking about you, the person who they are all staring at, the person that they are listening to drop words like dimes, but they are, instead, thinking about themselves. Audiences are selfish, so give them a reason to be. He could make millions selling that idea.

Meanwhile, folded in an envelope, was the check that had been handed him before he went on. It felt like precious cargo. It was all coming together now, he thought. Finally a way to deeply monetize this adventure that had started when Max W picked him up on the side of the highway in his Jeep all those years ago: Max's words were the currency and he had truly become the art.

Thinking this, Max smiled and laughed as he walked down the city streets. Jesus, even he was beginning to believe his own bullshit.

It was a perfect day. Bright blue skies and no humidity, a light breeze blowing off the ocean. Max walked and he walked and soon he found himself approaching Union Square Park and he went in past the people playing chess at small tables and to a bench where he sat down.

He thought about calling Susannah, telling her what a victory this all was, but he decided against it, not yet anyway. He wanted to keep it to himself for now. He wanted to savor it. The moment, the day, the fat check, the feeling of being in the city, the place he used to feel outside of it all, Tiny Tim looking through a window, and now he was not only inside it, but had also transcended it. A feeling of intense superiority came over him as he watched people moving through the park, hustling everywhere; the big, baggy hustle that was America and that he had figured out. It was all coming together now. He had fooled everyone, hadn't he? Well, maybe not Detective Scott, but what was she going to do? There was no case. The coroner said so.

Sitting in the park, a distant memory came to him, a time he had sat either on this bench or one like it. Across the way he had spotted a girl, a fellow traveler, and she saw him and his big bag and gave him a weak wave. Union Square Park was a common meeting place for crusty punks. He went over to her and they were instantly into it, talking a language only their kind understood. It was like being in a faraway country and spotting a fellow American. She was skinny and pretty with her hair, like his, falling down either side of her face in long brown dreadlocks. They smoked a joint she had and then Dumpster-dived for dinner behind the Union Square Café until they were chased off by someone coming out of the kitchen. That night, they fucked furtively on a bench in Battery Park, wrapped in blankets and looking out to the Statue of Liberty across the water. They slept curled up in the dark park, and when he woke, she was gone.

Max tried to remember her name now. Lauren maybe?

It didn't matter. In a long life, people pass in and out. *Funny,* he thought, *who it is we choose to have stay.*

MAX HAD DINNER THAT NIGHT at Marea, an expensive seafood place on Central Park South right next to his hotel. He was able to get a seat at the crowded bar and he ate things he knew he could never find in Vermont: an octopus grilled on a cedar plank; a sampling of different crudos; followed by a whole branzino that the bartender presented to him dead and uncooked, before returning it to the kitchen for roasting. He drank vodka martinis and he loved this kind of food. The freshest fish imaginable, prepared simply. It gave him a buzz.

Afterward, Max walked out of the restaurant and took out his phone. He stood on the sidewalk, people walking by him, and dialed Susannah. It rang and went to voice mail. He looked at the time. Weird, he thought, though maybe she was in the shower. He waited and called again and it went straight to voice mail.

Max sent her a text. *Where are u?*

He walked across the street and past the horses and carriages all lined up waiting for tourists. The horses looked sad and dirty. Max sat on a bench against the granite wall that separated the park from the street and texted Susannah again. More silence.

Now he texted Freddy the same question, and the response came right back. *Sleeping over Ivan's.*

Where's Mom? Max typed.

IDK. Home?

Max relaxed a bit. She hadn't made another run, for she wouldn't have gone without Freddy. Still, it wasn't like Susannah not to respond. Sometimes she would leave her phone charging in the kitchen and go do something, take a bath, say, but that was about it. Otherwise it was always with her and as with him, unless he was in class, an extension of her hand.

Max pulled up his itinerary on his phone. He was scheduled to be on an eleven a.m. flight tomorrow, a nod to leisure that schedule, sleep in and have room-service breakfast and then a car to whisk him to JFK for the hour-long flight to Burlington. Maybe he should just go back tonight, he thought. The idea didn't have a ton of appeal, but it would only take a minute to pack his bag and leave the hotel. It was still early.

Max called the airline, but the last flight of the night had already left, though if he wanted, they could move him up in the morning.

"What time?"

"Six-fifty a.m.," the woman said.

"I'll take it."

He then called the number for the car service that Goldman provided him and changed his pickup time. With those arrangements done, he returned to his hotel and that high, gilded suite they had rented him. He wrote Susannah again and again—no answer. He lay on top of the bedcovers with only his sneakers kicked off. He rented a movie on the television, some thriller with Tom Cruise, but barely paid attention to it.

Max found himself growing angry with Susannah. Today was an unmitigated triumph and tonight should have been a night of celebration, something he could have told her about over the phone, and maybe they could have done something fun tomorrow night to mark the occasion. Instead he was worried about her, or what she might have done. She could really be fucking selfish, he thought. Unable to escape her own head, she could never see the bigger picture. Look at all he had done for her, and for Freddy. What had she done for him? Introduced him to Lydia? Anyone could have done that.

Max climbed out of bed. He got on the floor and started doing push-ups. Up and down and up and down until his arms ached and his breathing came fast and shallow.

He stood and went to the window, his hands on his hips. He looked out to the park below in the dark, the street in front of it full of people. There was nothing to be done tonight, he decided.

Max slept fitfully, waking at times to look at his phone to see if she'd responded, but there was nothing. He woke at five and had coffee and fruit brought to the room. He then showered and fifteen minutes later he was in a black town car heading to JFK, just another wealthy traveler driving against the traffic to escape town.

Before the flight even took off, Max was asleep. Bright sunlight streaming through the rectangular window on his face woke him somewhere over Vermont. He looked out the window, and below he could see the sea of green and the undulating ridges of the Green Mountains, all of it from this height appearing wild and unspoiled. He rubbed his eyes and felt the down-nose of the descent.

Fifteen minutes later Max was out in front of the terminal. One of the things to love about Vermont: no wait for a cab. He came out the sliding doors and signaled to a half-asleep-looking guy sitting in a green Prius sedan that said GREEN CAB on the side and moments later Max was on his way back to his house. It was eight a.m.

The first thing Max noticed when the cab pulled up front was the Volkswagen parked in the driveway. The angle was such that the car was practically sideways, the tires turned sharply to the left.

Max handed the driver a twenty and said, "That's all set," and bounded out of the car with his bag. He came up the porch and he was going to look for his keys but tried the handle first and the door opened.

Max took the bag off his shoulder and came into the foyer, leaving his luggage there, looked into the living room, which appeared unlived in, and then into the kitchen. His eyes took it in. An empty wineglass on the counter but otherwise nothing amiss.

He went back down the hallway and climbed the stairs. Their bedroom door was ajar and he opened it slowly and silently, as if he expected to find a crime scene, which was ludicrous, he knew, but he did it anyway, and as if responding to the slight creak of the wooden door, Susannah stirred where she lay in the bed but did not wake.

Max walked to the bedside. She had the covers half-on, one naked long leg exposed, her panties hiked up and one cheek of her ass out. He felt his anger, his fear, falling away and he reached down for her hair, which was down, and slid his fingers through it. She rolled over.

Susannah looked up at him. She looked confused and jacked up, as if it had been a long night. She had worn makeup, he saw, the smear of lipstick on her upper lip, and this surprised him, since she rarely wore lipstick, unless they were going out for something special. Eyeliner, yes, but lipstick, no.

"Hey."

"Why didn't you answer my texts?"

"I lost my phone. I found it right before I crashed. It was late. I didn't want to bother you."

"I wouldn't have been bothered," said Max, though he didn't believe her.

She sat up, leaned against the pillows. She pushed her hair out of her face. She was beautiful: the red hair falling around her face, those big, sad eyes, rubbing them with her hands.

"Where were you last night?"

"What?"

"I mean, you went out. Where did you go?"

"Why are you interrogating me?"

"It's a simple question, Susannah."

"None of your questions are simple."

"Well, here's a simple one then." Max's voice rose a little. "Where are the car keys? I need to move it. You left it sideways in the middle of the driveway."

Susannah waved toward the clothes on the floor, a trail of her undressing. "My pockets, I don't know."

Max turned around and stormed over to where her jeans lay on the floor. He thrust his hand in the right front pocket and pulled a business card out of it. His heart sunk when he read it.

Detective Dolores Scott, Vermont State Police.

Max held it to his face, as if not believing what he was seeing. Susannah, in the meantime, had rolled away from him, her face pressed back into the pillow, her body curled up in the fetal position, pulling the covers up and around her, as if by doing so he might go away.

Max went to the bed, grabbed her shoulder, and pulled her toward him, onto her back.

"What the fuck?" Susannah said.

He threw the card at her. "What is this? What did you say to her, Susannah?"

Susannah reached down and took the card off the top of the comforter where it had fluttered to a stop.

She sighed. "I didn't say anything to her."

"Why do you have this?"

"She forced it on me."

"When, Susannah? When?"

"Relax, please, okay? Yesterday, okay? I was in the co-op. I didn't talk to her. She just gave it to me."

"She just gave it to you."

"Yes, she gave it to me."

Max walked away from Susannah. He went to the window and looked out to the backyard, the majestic peonies lining it, the perfectly green yard in the morning light. He wished he had hair so he could rip it out. He didn't know what to believe.

"Tell me everything." He had his back to her. "Every single fucking word."

Susannah started to cry. "Why are you doing this?"

"Just tell me." He didn't turn around.

"It was nothing. I was shopping. She came up to me. 'I bet you have a story to tell,' she said. I told her I didn't tell stories, she left me alone."

"That was it?"

"Yes, I swear. That was it."

Max sat down on the bed, facing away from Susannah. In a moment, she rose up and her arms draped around his neck and he felt her bare breasts against his back.

"Hey," she said softly, "I would never do anything."

Max nodded. "Okay," he said, coming down from it. "Okay." As he thought about it further, he did believe Susannah. He believed she hadn't said anything to Detective Scott. But he also knew that this meant he was right about the detective, about that moment when she got into her car in the parking lot outside his office and squinted up to where he stood. She wasn't going to quit, not yet. The biggest liability he had was behind him right now, her hands on his chest, her mouth inches from his ear.

In a couple of days they would go to the ocean, to the beautiful house he had rented for the three of them. *This will give you time to think,* Max told himself. He would know what to do when the time came. The point was not to be rash.

IN THE FOLLOWING DAYS, A simple détente came over them. The vacation was all that they talked about, the seafood they would eat, the long days on the beach, the feel of salt water on skin.

"The sunsets," said Max, "are spectacular."

The more they talked, the more normal it all seemed. Susannah surprised herself with how easily she could compartmentalize this experience. How easily she could pretend they were like everyone else in the prime of their lives. Max was acting like his old self, full of life and stories, and while they didn't fuck, every time she saw him in the kitchen or anywhere else, his hands were on her, knowing and searching, strong fingers on the rise of her hip.

Thirty-six years old and Susannah had never been on a proper vacation. She wasn't counting a night away with the girls, which she had done a few times back in the city days, some quick get out of town, or the few times she and Max had found a way to slip off, also usually just for one night. It was so amazingly American, all of it, the idea that it was summer and they were going to pack up the car and go to the beach, hot sand between their toes, wet sand stuck to their ankles.

Freddy was bringing his friend Cal, a kid who was even more re-served and sullen than Freddy was. But the prospect of this made the trip palatable for Freddy. Max and Susannah were determined to get the most out of it—they took possession of the rental at noon on

Saturday—so that meant leaving at the ass crack of dawn, which Susannah didn't mind at all. After three days of thinking about it constantly, she really wanted to go.

She surprised herself by how she was feeling. All of a sudden she loved the whole idea of this trip. The house, with all of them in it, had begun to feel like a prison. In the early morning as Freddy and Cal slid into the backseat with their headphones on and their closed eyes, and Max got behind the wheel and backed out of the driveway, she was almost manic with excitement. She was the kid in the car, the one who could hardly wait.

It rained in Vermont, but by the time they reached New Hampshire, bright sun was in the sky, and at a stop to use the restrooms, the heat hit her hard as soon as the car door opened. Summer.

Susannah liked the feeling of driving to the sea. She imagined the road was a river or a tide with an undertow, pulling her to where she was meant to go. Even the heavy traffic they hit in Boston—some construction and a minor accident backing things up for an hour—couldn't quell her enthusiasm. She did have a moment when the traffic stopped in the tunnel under the city when she felt it coming on, everyone else in the car oblivious of how they were underground and couldn't move. Everyone, she should say, with the exception of her husband, who looked over and saw the strained look on her face and read it correctly.

"There's nothing above us," he said.

"I thought we were under the harbor," she said, considering all that water rushing in from a sudden breach, how it would consume all the cars and make them rise at once while, paradoxically, or inversely, the occupants would sink. She imagined the four of them tumbling upside down like astronauts, peaceful in the minutes before they died.

"No," Max said. "Not here. This just goes under a park."

Susannah took a breath.

But then she could see the mouth of the tunnel and the light, and like that, they were out and south of the city, though the traffic grew heavier, if that was possible. It was stop-and-go. Midmorning.

She tried to remind herself of the lightness she had felt earlier in the morning. What a North Star the very idea of this vacation was, not as much when Max had told her it was happening, but in the last few days, when she began to dream of the beach.

She said to herself, *My mind is telling me not to be upset. It's just my mind, a separate thing. Doing what it does.*

But the traffic broke and so did her sour mood. The landscape changed. Now on either side of the two-lane highway were scrubby pine trees, small and bent and growing out of sand. Susannah rolled down the window for a moment and the air was warm and smelled of salt and the sea.

They hit traffic again before the bridge, but now Susannah didn't care at all, and when they rose on the great arc over the canal and onto Cape Cod, she turned to the boys and said excitedly, "Look at the boats."

The water below was bluer than Max's eyes, and big ships moved down the canal and away from them and toward the open ocean.

But her real joy was saved for the house, this splurge of a rental house. In Wellfleet they left Route 6 and drove down this road that ran high above the ocean. They turned off down a sandy path, and there the house sat, perched precariously, it seemed, on top of a dune. The longest staircase Susannah could imagine ran from the deck of the house down to the beach. The beach was far below, at least several hundred feet.

In front of them, as they took it in moments after getting out of the car, was the huge expanse of wide-open Atlantic, sparkling like knives in the bright sun. It might have been the most beautiful view Susannah had ever seen.

After they unpacked the car, the boys ran through the house, which was small, but that didn't matter because they had the big deck and the whole world outside to play in. Susannah made sandwiches in the kitchen and put them in a small cooler and Max carried this and four chairs out the door.

"I'll be down in a minute," Susannah said. "Need to use the bathroom."

"We can wait for you," Max said.

"No, no, go ahead."

From the window, Susannah watched as they all descended the long staircase to the great expanse of national seashore. She pulled out her phone and taking a card out of her pocket, she dialed a Vermont number. *Pick up*, she thought. *Pick up*.

On the third ring, a woman's gentle voice: "Detective Scott."

"This is Susannah Garcia," she said breathlessly.

"Susannah. Are you okay?"

"You told me I looked like I might have a story to tell."

"I remember."

"Google Maxwell Westmoreland from Charleston, South Carolina. My husband knew him and took his name. My husband's real name is Phil Wilbur. He says Maxwell Westmoreland is alive in Alaska. I think he's dead. I think he killed him like he killed David Hammer. And I think he might kill me. I have to go."

"Susannah, wait. Are you safe? Where are you?"

"For now. I have to go." Susannah hung up.

They spent the afternoon trying to bodysurf the large waves that crashed onto the beach. Susannah shrieked when each wave came in and she tried to outjump them, only sometimes feeling the brute force of the undertow picking her up and sending her spinning before pushing her up on the shore like driftwood, all of them laughing and sun-kissed and sandy and perfect.

That night they ate dinner outside at Mac's Shack in the village of Wellfleet, Susannah and Max slurping briny oyster after briny oyster and drinking sparkling wine while the two boys drank root beer and ate avocado rolls by the dozen. Then they had lobsters and corn, dipping the sweet, succulent meat into the golden butter while the breeze coming off the harbor blew warm and brackish.

After dinner, Max, acting on an intelligence tip from one of the waiters, drove them along the bay side, where the beaches were tidal and the waves nonexistent, but the sunsets spectacular. They stopped at the first beach they found. The boys didn't want to get out of the car, but Susannah wasn't having it, not tonight, and she forced them to, and while they weren't the only ones with this idea—the parking lot was full—it was hard not to love. They walked out into the soft sand and the sun, orange and big and from their perspective about two feet above the horizon.

They sat down on the sand. Freddy was on one side of her, and Max was on the other, Cal off next to Freddy. It was like watching a stop-motion movie, the sun bigger than she'd ever seen it, slowly sinking beyond the curve of the earth, leaving in its wake magnificent stripes of red, yellow, and purple.

She didn't want to leave. Susannah wanted to stay until the last wisp of light left the sky even though with the sun gone it had instantly gotten cold. Reluctantly, she rose and followed her husband and her son and his friend back the way they had come to the parking lot. If this was going to be her last day, she had picked a good one.

The boys went to their room, as if they were back at home.

Susannah knew it would be only moments before they were on their phones or the iPad, doing who knew what. It didn't matter where they were, and while she wished it did, she felt so completely close to whole tonight, she wasn't going to let anything get in the way of that feeling. Especially rules.

"Pour me something," she said lazily to Max in the kitchen. The kitchen was small and dated and campy and smelled like Grandma's house.

A moment later, he brought her a glass of white wine. He had one, too.

"Take me outside," said Susannah.

He laughed. "Okay."

They went out the screen door of the kitchen and it slapped closed behind them. They were on the wooden deck. The moon was out and had risen above the ocean, and when they looked out, it was still low but it was fat and its white light beat a path across the water toward them.

"Thank you," Susannah said.

"For what?"

"For this, for all of it."

"I like seeing you this way."

"Walk with me."

Looking to the left, she could see other houses, tucked here and there among the brush on the top of the dunes, houses lit with single lights, but to the right, the land rose up gradually away from their own. Off to the right of the deck was a small path in the sand, through thorny low bushes.

Susannah led Max on this, up a small slope in the dark, and they came through the brush and suddenly they were on top of the cliff, high above the beach, and the moonlight was bright enough that they could see the edge in front of them clearly. A small sign on the ground said WATCH YOUR STEP, NO GUARDRAIL.

She stopped here. Max came alongside her. Susannah looked down and even in the dark she could see how insanely far down it was, and she told herself to ignore it, to look straight ahead, to watch the stillness of the black beyond and the highway the moon beat across the ocean.

Max slid in next to her. She felt his arm come around her and she turned her head to his and he leaned down and his lips met her lips.

He looked at her hard, the way he did when he meant something. "Have you ever seen anything more beautiful?" She felt his arm stronger against her back, securing her.

"No," she said, and despite herself she started to tremble.

"Are you cold?"

"I'm fine." Susannah pointed south down the coast. "How do you get to that lighthouse?"

Max peered that way, as if studying it, then he took his arm away from her for a moment and stepped forward. "I think—"

She did it, pushed him as hard she could, slamming into him, then falling to the ground herself. The key was the surprise of it all, the push he wasn't expecting, the half stumble, the reach back but all his weight was moving forward and it was too late.

Susannah scrambled to her feet and watched him fall. His arms out, grabbing nothing but air. Max was falling away from her like a snow angel that disappears, until he was completely gone.

She was too far away to hear him hit the sand.

TWO
MONTHS
LATER

Detective Dolores Scott stood on the side of a mountain in the Adirondacks on a hot day in August. The wool of her uniform against her skin was driving her nuts, as it often did in summer. So was her hat. Shouldn't it have been cooler given how high they were? She became aware of the sweat in the place where her brim met her forehead, but she'd be damned if she let any of these New York State troopers in their gray uniforms know that. They all towered over her. And seemed fine in the heat.

"Bit out of your jurisdiction, Detective," the captain had said to her when they arrived at the house in the late morning, the least subtle thing ever, their arrival, a line of state troopers and vans moving down the only road that came through the small mountain valley and then up the long single-lane driveway.

"Just a bit," she said.

"You're sure he's here?"

"Oh, he's here."

She watched as the troopers spread out across the land, starting on the part that rose sharply up away from the right of the house, steep forest walls heading toward the summit. Of the six cadaver-sniffing dogs, five were German shepherds and one was a yellow Lab. A trooper held each one by a leash.

In front of her was the house, if you could call it that. It looked more like an Austrian inn.

"Can you believe people live like this?" she said to the captain from New York.

"I've seen enough of it." He walked away from her and over to where the land fell away, the long valley in front of him, mountains rising up all around.

Dolores Scott ignored him—she was used to it by now, all these men in law enforcement who were sexist and dismissive without even trying. It was part of the culture. Instead, she thought of Susannah while she listened for the bark of the dogs.

She thought of the call that came that day in July—not the first one that led her to this place—but the second one, the panic in Susannah's voice. The rush of words as she tried to explain what had happened, the sound of the wind blowing on the beach that made her hard to hear, the beach where Max lay broken and dead on his back.

Dolores stopped her. "Susannah, listen to me. Are there marks on him from you? Did you scratch him or anything?"

"No, no. I don't think so."

"Susannah. He jumped."

"What? What do you mean?"

"Susannah, Max jumped. He killed himself. Say it back to me." Susannah did.

"Now make the call. And say only that. He jumped, okay?"

"What do I tell Freddy?"

"The truth. That Max jumped. And why. You know why, Susannah, right?"

"Yes."

"Because I know everything, right? He was going to go away for a long time."

"Yes."

"Okay. Make the call."

I would have pushed that motherfucker off that cliff, too, Dolores thought. *Happily*.

The coroner ruled that the death was consistent with suicide (also with his being shoved), but after Susannah told the Massachusetts State Police what had happened, and Dolores backed it up with phone calls both to the state police and the Barnstable district attorney, no charges were filed. There was no case. Nothing could be proved. The path of least resistance, once again, was the right one. No one wants a fight that cannot be won. The DA ruled that Max had killed himself.

Remarkably, and a circumstance that surprised Dolores that it did not bring more attention to Susannah, Max's death was exactly 366 days after he had signed his contract with the University of Vermont and accepted a life insurance policy that came with the position. The policy was for $250,000 and did not cover suicide in the first year but did in subsequent years. Had Max leaped off a cliff the day before, Susannah wouldn't have gotten a thing.

Dolores learned all this a week later, sitting on the porch of that big house Susannah and Max had near the college. Susannah had made them tea. She looked surprisingly well. She looked rested. It was a warm day but a soft midsummer rain fell. Freddy ran up on the porch and past them, stopping only briefly to say hello before he went through the door and clomped up the stairs.

"He took it all okay," Dolores said, more of a statement than a question.

"Yes. He wants to go. Like me. He can't wait to leave."

"But he loved Max."

"Yes."

Dolores, watching Susannah, admired her, what a great beauty she was, and how under all that fragility, like a body under thin ice, lay the unbroken spine of a strong woman. *They can bend us*, Dolores thought, *but breaking us takes more than they got.*

Dolores saw Susannah steel herself, almost imperceptibly, before she spoke.

"But he's learning too young how fickle life is."

"What will you do?"

"Go back to New York. Get a place. Start over."

A few days later, Dolores had another conversation, on another porch, a block away with Joanie Hammer, who was also planning to move, but back South, to Atlanta, where she had family.

Dolores told her what she knew and what she didn't know. She said that she thought Max had killed David but she could probably never prove it. She told Joanie she had discovered that Max was operating under an assumed name and an assumed identity, that he had never gone to art school, and that he had probably never even graduated high school. He had used another man's transcripts from CalArts, a man she believed Max had killed many years ago.

David must have discovered this somehow, and desperate to keep it secret, Max had killed David. Dolores told Joanie she was determined to find out what had happened to the original Max W, and that she was working with the New York State Police to get a warrant to search the house and land in the Adirondacks.

"Why are you telling me this?" Joanie said.

"I thought you should know."

"Will it bring David back?"

"No."

"And Max won't pay for it either."

"No."

"Then fuck you."

"I'm sorry." Dolores meant it, she was.

"I know. I'm sorry, too. I know you're just doing your job."

Now, standing in front of the great house framed by higher mountains, Dolores watched the policemen and their dogs as they fanned out across the woods. They moved methodically, a phalanx of cops, dogs bent toward the earth, through the trees.

MIDAFTERNOON, DOWNHILL FROM THE HOUSE, on a small plateau before the land plummeted down toward the rural highway far below, the dogs began to bark as if their lives depended on it. First one and then they all converged on one spot between two tall pine trees. They dug as if they were searching for a cure until they were pulled off and then they kept barking until they were led away.

Troopers taped off the spot and within an hour the remains of Maxwell Westmoreland, missing for twenty-plus years, were exhumed. Identification would have to wait for dental records, but there was no question who lay there.

"Well, you were right, Scott," the New York captain said to her on the porch. "Congratulations."

"There's no winners in this one." She meant it.

ONE
YEAR
LATER

THEY HAD A NEW LOFT, on Mercer Street in SoHo, a funky place with high ceilings and big windows and lots of light that streamed in all day. It was lined with art and design and architecture books, in bookcases that rose from the floor to the ceiling, and the two bedrooms were alcoves separated from the rest of the space by curtains. The kitchen had an old French cast-iron stove with tiny ovens and heavy doors that was far more charming than it was practical.

The apartment belonged to an artist that Lydia knew who was on a Fulbright in Italy for a year and willing to sublet cheap for the right person who would look after the dog, a Jack Russell named Pablo, so quiet he was practically invisible, spending all day sleeping on the couch, often half under blankets. Susannah loved the place, and on this night in September she knew it would come to an end—they had four months left—but she couldn't think about that now. She was learning to live in the moment.

She forced herself to eat, more for Freddy than anything else, some Chinese takeout brought to the door. Then they dressed. Freddy had put up a fight at first but gave in eventually. She marveled at him when he emerged from his bedroom with the outfit she had chosen for him: a black suit coat over a black T-shirt, dark jeans, and white sneakers. He had pierced his ears a few weeks before, and he wore silver stud earrings in each, and his hair had grown longer, dark and rich and full and falling almost to his shoulders in the back.

"You are so handsome," she said.

"Quit it."

Susannah wore a black dress, of course. Tight. That morning she had gotten her hair blown out and she splurged and had her makeup done, too, as if she were getting married or something.

They rode an Uber uptown, a black Chevy Suburban. Freddy had his earphones on. Susannah's phone rang and it was Rose, the noise behind her promising what was to come, her voice full and excited.

"Hey, girl," Rose shouted, "you ready?"

"I am," Susannah said calmly.

"Where are you?"

Susannah looked past the driver and out the windshield in front. "Crawling up Sixth."

"Well, get here. Awesome crowd, honey."

"On my way." And Susannah was, in more ways than one. She felt that.

The Garabedian Gallery took up the first three floors of a prewar granite building on Madison Avenue. The Suburban double-parked out front and Susannah and Freddy got out. For a moment, before the entrance, Susannah stopped, and Freddy stopped next to her. She reached down and took his hand in hers and he didn't pull away, but allowed this. Her eyes ran up the building to the second floor, the smaller of the two main galleries. She could see people huddled together, shapes and champagne flutes extended. She took a deep breath and said to Freddy, "Let's do this."

They came in the main entrance and then over to the large elevator and rode up one floor. The elevator opened right in the middle of the gallery, polished wood floors as far as you could see, white walls, white ceilings, the large windows on the front. And there, right in front of them, was a giant photo of Susannah next to the words:

Susannah Garcia
The Max Paintings
Oil, Acrylic, Mixed Media

Lydia, with her nearly uncanny ability to know how to move around a room, got to her first. There Lydia was, all flowing white, taking Susannah's hand, and saying to her, "Darling, it's already a hit. You are ascendant."

For six months, and for the first time since art school, Susannah had painted. It was as if something had broken within her, and all day when Freddy was in school, and sometimes deep into the night, she painted in a state of near mania. The more she put on canvas, abstract portraits of Max, MURDER written boldly in bright red paint on some of them, the less she felt afraid, and the less she felt alone.

It was Rose's idea that Lydia come look at them. Susannah was smart enough to know that while Lydia's over-the-top enthusiasm was about the paintings, it was more about Max. He had become more famous, or infamous perhaps, in death than he had been in life. A *Vanity Fair* article from the winter after his death, titled "A Modern-Day Talented Mr. Ripley Exits the Stage," told the story of his meteoric rise from homeless teenager to art-world darling. Everyone was talking about it.

So what if Susannah was Yoko Ono to his John Lennon? Did it matter?

Not tonight, Susannah decided. She leaned into the party as if it were a breeze.

"So many people are dying to meet you," Lydia said.

"Bring me to them."